"If you like your space opera rough and tumble, this one is right up your alley. Etheridge weaves a complex tapestry of politics, war, and religion, all stitched together with plenty of fast and deadly action."

—**Steve Perry** on *Legend of the Duelist*

"Action-packed SF adventure . . . There are battle scenes galore, [as well as] intrigue."

—**Kliatt** on *Legend of the Duelist*

"This book is loaded with martial arts, colorful characters . . . Etheridge, an ex-submariner . . . brings military expertise and knowledge of governmental business to his writing."

—*The Oregonian* on *The First Duelist*

Ace Books by Rutledge Etheridge

LEGEND OF THE DUELIST
THE FIRST DUELIST
AGENT OF DESTRUCTION
AGENT OF CHAOS
BROTHER JOHN

BROTHER JOHN

RUTLEDGE ETHERIDGE

ACE BOOKS, NEW YORK

This is a work of fiction. Names, characters, places, and incidents either are the product of the author's imagination or are used fictitiously, and any resemblance to actual persons, living or dead, business establishments, events, or locales is entirely coincidental.

BROTHER JOHN

An Ace Book / published by arrangement with
the author

PRINTING HISTORY
Ace mass-market edition / August 2001

Visit our Web site at
www.penguinputnam.com

Check out the ACE Science Fiction & Fantasy newsletter
and much more on the Internet at Club PPI!

ISBN: 0-441-00839-9

ACE®
Ace Books are published by The Berkley Publishing Group,
a division of Penguin Putnam Inc.,
375 Hudson Street, New York, New York 10014.
ACE and the "A" design
are trademarks belonging to Penguin Putnam Inc.

PRINTED IN THE UNITED STATES OF AMERICA

10 9 8 7 6 5 4 3 2 1

PROLOGUE

*O*F THE THOUSAND *billion human beings living and dying among the fifteen hundred worlds of the Great Domain, fewer than thirty thousand bore the title Duelist.*

The name was first applied to a small band of men and women who, in the late twenty-second century, fought alongside Admiral Simon Barrow to pave the way for humankind's expansion into an unknown, waiting galaxy. Simon Barrow and his followers were successful. Thus was born the Great Domain.

By the twenty-fourth century the original meaning of the term "Duelist" had been lost in antiquity. The name now represented not a quest, but a profession. The powerful Duelist Union provided a loose unity for the men and women of this calling—who arose from all the diverse peoples and the rich variety of cultures flourishing among the worlds of the Great Domain.

But the work of Admiral Simon Barrow was not en-

tirely forgotten. Many of the legends and the traditions which grew around the First Duelist survived him and assumed a life of their own. Perhaps most important was the credo that Barrow had lived by, and which found new meaning with every generation of Duelists: Go. Reach. Do.

Modern-day Duelists were heroes, rogues, knights errant, kill-for-hires, villains, entertainers, mercenaries, bounty hunters. In a word, they were individualists.

But above all, they were combat artists—the finest ever produced, or dreamt of, by the human race.

I JANUS

It seemed there was no way for the boy giant to avoid another fight. He hadn't provoked the man; he hadn't even laughed at him, and that wasn't easy. Aside from wearing the dumbest and most comical expression John had ever seen, the man had hair that was dyed white and shaped into a ball that sat on an otherwise shaved scalp. The hairstyle was something new from Earth, John decided, or from some other irrelevant place.

And that wasn't all. The man's neck was actually wider than his head. Just above his Adam's apple he was wearing a studded leather collar that matched the slightly smaller ones around his forearms. The man was bare-chested and wore tight green trousers spangled with gold. These days there weren't many visitors to the world of Janus, and few of those ever ventured into Dennis Town. Of those who did, none had ever looked anything like this man. He was a very odd creature. But John did not laugh at him.

By contrast John was shaggy-haired, jut-jawed, and big-eared. His nose was broad and straight. As always, he was dressed in dusty brown work clothes. If there was anything peculiar about him it was that he was seven feet seven inches tall, and weighed four hundred and eighty two pounds. And his family name was Biggle. But the people in Dennis Town were used to all of that, because the Biggles had been a part of Dennis Town since its founding as a mining camp three generations before. They were like the land itself: there no matter what, taken for granted, and not always safe to approach too closely.

What John had done, and all he'd done, was to nod politely at the stranger and ask Miss Lennox behind the bar if she needed any work done. He always asked, because Miss Lennox usually paid him right away, and in cash. And doing some work for her gave him an excuse to stay away from his grandfather Gus for a while. Gus was always the reason he came here. But Miss Lennox said no, there was no work. So John took a deep breath and promised himself that no matter what the odd stranger did, he wouldn't get angry. This time he would remain in complete control. It took him a few seconds to settle his mind, and then he turned for Gus's table. That's when it started

"You have to fight me now," the man said. "Now it's time to fight me." Someone might have said in the same tone, "Excuse me, you wanted to know when it's noon. Well, it is, just now." It sounded more like a friendly reminder, than a threat.

John nodded politely again, this time adding a smile, and continued on for his grandfather's table. The man ran around him and blocked his way. That happened three different times. After the third time John looked down at him with a blank expression. The man grunted out something that didn't sound like words. John tried turning his face away and standing there quietly, harmless as a dove, waiting for the man to get bored and go back to his drink. The man reached up and slapped the back of John's head. And giggled.

"I hate this," the young giant muttered under his breath. "I really do."

"What's the matter with you, John?" Miss Lennox asked. "Go on and give him what he's asking for, and let's everybody dance." Amy Lennox was Wilfred Manley's manager, and the only employee, of The Pit. She was short and shaped like a barrel, formidably strong, and bore a permanent squint from years of wearing spectacles that were missing a lens. The passions of her life were money and the thousands of ways it could be made. Tonight was almost too easy. A good fight followed by a hard dance meant alcohol, and plenty of it. Business promised to be so good that Wilfred Manley might give her a bonus, if she caught him in the right frame of mind. With practiced fingers she counted the cash in the drawer and wrote down the amount. She'd count again at the close of business and show Manley the comparison.

"Are you sure you want that, Miss Lennox?" John asked. "Last time you made me pay for damage even though I never started it."

"You're not starting anything, John," she told him. "It's all right, I promise."

John shook his head, undecided. Besides not wanting to bother with pounding the stranger, he was thinking about Ko Kim, who was outside at the window with her ear pressed against it. Ko Kim was probably the one person who really cared about him, and she hated for John to fight. "Maybe I'll just drag him behind back and thrash him there, if he won't leave me alone," he said. Show no fear, Gus always told him. Confidence, that's what makes them back down. He hoped it would work this time the way it usually did.

"Now," the man said, grinning. "Fight me now." He was large, only a head shorter than John and a hundred fifty pounds or so lighter. But he was far better muscled, and John had read enough and heard enough stories to know what he was: a circus fighter. One of the legendary Duelists. But not so proud anymore, and that could be for a hundred different reasons. Most often circus fighters were drunks or druggies. Or were done in by a bad wife or a bad husband. There were probably dozens of reasons a Duelist might turn circus fighter and none of them mattered very much to John. What mattered was that they were unbelievably dangerous. Big or small, man or woman, reigning champion or disgraced, they were still Duelists. The best ones were so good they could kill you in their sleep. That's what Gus always said. "They'll kill you, John, big as you are. Easy as squashing a fly, and they don't even have to wake up to do it."

To John that seemed like an awfully humiliating way to die. Losing a fight was bad enough, he supposed, although he'd never lost one. Being killed in a fight was worse, of course. But losing a fight and being killed by someone so much better than you that he could sleep through the whole thing and squash you like a snoring man swats a fly . . . that was as embarrassing as it gets. The best Duelists would do that to prove how superior they were, according to Gus. Circus fighters weren't the best, though. They'd come down low. They'd fight a bear, a pig, a big snake, or anything. To the death, anywhere, for money. They'd even fight a boy who hadn't done anything more offensive than being bigger than anyone else. That, and the slap in the head, made him angry.

But he wasn't going to fight if he didn't have to. Not with Ko Kim listening at the window.

Amy Lennox didn't answer his question. Instead she leaned over the bar and motioned for him to put his head down to her level. She whispered in his ear and told him what had been going on before he came in. John nodded and straightened up. He could have figured most of it out for himself. Little people always thought that big people were stupid. It was probably the same everywhere, not just in Dennis Town or on Janus, but wherever there were big people and little people.

"There won't be any damages. But if there are, I'll pay." This was said by the sharply dressed woman Miss Lennox had pointed to and said that no one had seen before that day. She said her name was Iris. Iris had walked into The Pit about an hour after the circus fighter. Miss Lennox had said no one was fooled, though. Two newcomers on the same day had to be together. And the fighter didn't start any trouble until after Iris got there.

"Why don't we do this?" John asked the man. "I'll say I'm sorry for bothering you, and I'll buy you and your friend something to drink. Then I have to go, because Ko Kim's waiting for me and Gus outside. Is that all right?"

He didn't think it would be, and his grandfather

made sure of that. "You have money, John?" Gus called out. "Where'd you get any money?"

John shook his head. What was wrong with the old man, anyway? Gus had raised his mother and taken John in as an infant, when both his parents died. Gus was his own blood, but liquor made him do crazy things. "I'll work for it, Gus. Miss Lennox always lets me work."

"Well, then!" Gus stood up from his regular table and spread his arms like a sheep-tender calling his flock. "My friends are more deserving than any worthless ex-Duelist. Lennox, we'll all go again, if you please." Thirty-eight men and women, most of them miners without jobs, applauded.

"No, that's not what I'm saying," John said. "All I want to do—"

"Fight me now," the man repeated.

"And not only for damages," Iris said. She craned her neck back to look John in the face. "How would you like a little money for yourself?" She followed John's gaze as he turned to the window, where Ko Kim was standing with her left ear pressed against the glass. Iris added, "You can use the money to pay for that pretty little whore outside."

"Ma'am," John said. "I really don't think you should—"

"Listen," Iris said. "I've got a hundred right here to give somebody. If you don't take it, Cyclone Tom will." She held the money out to the circus fighter. "Woman, Tom? Pretty woman?" Again she pointed at Ko Kim, at the window. "Whore," she added.

Tom grinned with gleaming teeth at her, and at Ko Kim.

Iris said to John, "I'll make it three hundred to you, if Cyclone Tom falls."

The circus fighter grunted and reached for the money. He said, "Whore." And that ended all conversation. John smiled. Not because he was happy; the smile was part of something Ko Kim had taught him. It was called "acting."

"Fair enough," he said. He was still smiling when he swung.

The man never saw it coming. John's left arm came up in an open backhand to the man's ear that made the fighter's eyes glaze over. They were even now, but it couldn't end just yet. The fighter had reflexes, and they were coming into play. John stepped back and ducked beneath a double-fisted sweep aimed at his head. He lifted the fighter, with no strain or hurry, and threw him six feet to an empty table. The table and the man tumbled for another six feet. Iris screamed and kicked at John's shins. John ignored her and walked to the table. He stood quietly while the fighter pulled himself to his feet.

He said to Iris, "I believe Cyclone Tom has fallen. You owe me three hundred, ma'am. Want to bet it?"

The fighter straightened up, keeping the table between them. The swelling below his ear was bad already, and was going to get worse. He glared up at John and closed a wide hand around the top of a chair.

Gus called out, "If he picks it up, boy, throw him through the window. That woman can buy Manley a new one." With both hands waving he bellowed, "Ko Kim, you get out of the way! Go on, get away from there!" He coughed until a long breath was gone and stood unsteadily to cross the room to John. "Don't worry about her," he said. "Or her, either," he added, aiming a glare at Iris. "I'll watch your back."

Cyclone Tom wasn't moving, except to turn his head and see the people there laughing at him. "That wasn't good," he said, turning back to John. "That hurt. And Iris promised they'd like me—"

"Tom!" Iris ran to him and put her hands to his face. One touched the swelling, while the other slid over his mouth. "You can be quiet now," she said. "It's all right to be quiet." She was fifty or so, with long thin fingers.

"But that hurt and I want to ask—"

"I know," Iris said in a soothing voice. "You want to break the boy in half."

"No, that's not it. It wasn't fun, like you said. And I don't understand why he—"

"I'll explain everything, Tom. But first you want to be quiet. That's what you want to do. You're the boss, remember? Do what you want to do."

The fighter's eyes seemed to clear. He nodded his head. Iris dropped her hands.

John stared down at her. He was disgusted, and the acting was over. "This was all your idea, wasn't it? You take a poor, addled man and make him get hurt for you."

Iris arched an eyebrow and smiled. In a stage-loud voice she said, "What was that? You say Cyclone Tom is stupid? Did you hear him, Tom? He says you're stupid!"

Now the fighter showed real pain. "That's not true! I'm not stupid!"

"Sir, I never said you were," John said. "Look, addled means you've been hit too many times. That's all it means. It isn't your fault, it's just a condition some people have."

"He means stupid people!" Iris shouted. "There! He said it again!"

"I'll kill you!" Tom stamped his feet, but did not move after Iris put a restraining hand on his chest. He bent his head to one side and mewled. Iris scratched at his neck.

She went on as smoothly as if she'd written out the whole incident in advance. "Young man, you have provoked one of the greatest fighters in the Great Domain. On eight hundred worlds—eight hundred! Do you know how many there are who practice the combat arts at his level? Do you have any idea who this man is? This is Cyclone Tom! A Duelist! If you have any sense you'll apologize quick. And you owe me your life, for stopping him when I did."

"And you," Gus said from behind John, "owe my grandson three hundred." He turned to the crowd and spoke as theatrically as Iris. "She's right about one thing, though. He's a Duelist. Hell, anybody can tell that. And you all saw it, right? My boy whipped a Duelist! One of the best on eight hundred worlds!"

When the murmuring and the glass-banging died down, John said, "No, Gus, that's not right. He was a Duelist. Maybe. And even if he was, he's a circus fighter now. It's not the same." Amy Lennox darted from table to table with a pitcher in each hand, filling the glasses that were held out to her.

"You never go anywhere, boy," Gus said as the round of drinks brought on a round of murmuring. The people there had seen something few had ever seen. They'd seen a Duelist beaten. No one was going to take

that away from them, not even the one who'd done the
beating. With crowd support Gus could be charming
and smooth. "So we're not angry at you, because nobody expects you to know what goes on with life. But
I've heard of this Cyclone Tom. They say he was about
as good as anyone gets, being a Duelist. When I heard
about him he was working in a traveling show up at
Portside. He killed a lion, twisted its neck till it went
off like thunder."

"He wasn't *in* that show," Iris said indignantly. "He
was that show. Now he's chosen to elevate himself to
solo artist again. And I'm his manager." She wheeled
around and craned her neck up at John again. "If I
hadn't stepped in just now, out of respect for this es-
tablishment and"—she gestured widely—"these fine
people here, Cyclone Tom would have . . . young man,
don't you dare turn away from me when I'm talking to
you! You come back here!"

John knew she wasn't talking to him, she was talking to whoever had money to bet. He stopped in the
doorway and looked outside. Ko Kim was gone, but he
thought he knew where she'd be. Turning back to Gus,
he said, "I came to tell you that Ling-Ling should be in
foal by tonight. Ko Kim and I are taking the flyer in
case we have to bring her to Dr. Samuels. Do you want
a ride home?"

"What about the three hundred, boy?"

"I don't want it," John said. "Not that way."

"That's fine," Gus said. His hands, once hard as steel
but now soft and scarred, held on to each other with a
show of mutual affection. "We need a few things. Not
me, but you and the twins and Ko Kim. But don't

worry, I'll take care of them by myself. Tell Ko Kim not to wait for me."

John turned to go.

"Wait!" Iris called out. "Young man, this is not over. You owe Cyclone Tom and these people an apol—"

Outside the sunlight was brilliant, forcing John to walk head-down. As he rounded the old wooden building and headed for the rear he walked out of what little moving air there was, and the heat dropped on him like a scalding blanket. Even in the narrow band of morning shade it was oppressive. And it stank. The motionless air was holding on to the stench of urine and vomit from the past night's revelry, dark patches on the side of the building that were still steaming. John pulled off his shirt and used it to mop away the sweat.

The alley was a fifteen-foot gap between The Pit and what had once been a competitor but was now a fire-blackened half shell, long closed down and abandoned. As he passed through it he heard, "Ho, Big John!"

He knew who that was. Only one person called him that and meant it in friendship. He shielded his eyes and looked up at a second-story window. That was a reflex, and he regretted it. The window she stood in was more of a frame than anything else. A picture frame painted yellow and white like flowers, that put her on display from her knees to the top of her head.

"Ho, Mary," he called back. He couldn't look away now, or she'd be embarrassed. But he wished she didn't have to stand naked in the window like that all day, just because Mr. Manley thought someone might walk by and decide to spend some money. "Have you seen Ko Kim?" he asked. "She might have come around this way looking for Gus's flyer."

"Can you come up and talk for a while?"

"No, Ling-Ling's ready to foal."

"Already? Well, the flyer's around back and Ko Kim said to tell you she's running home and don't pick her up. I think that's what she was trying to tell me. She didn't look right. Is she getting sick again?" Mary had a beautiful face. People always mentioned her eyes when they were talking about her, no matter what else they might have in mind to say. Her eyes were so blue they were almost purple, and the whites were usually so bright they'd seem like they were shining all on their own. They weren't shining today, but it could have been that John was sweating and his own eyes felt ragged and blurry. He guessed he just couldn't see what was really there.

"I don't know, Mary. She might be."

"That poor woman. They ever catch the men who did that to her?"

"No."

"Well, I hope they do. You were fighting again, weren't you? I can hear them celebrating downstairs. Looks like another busy day."

"It wasn't really a fight. Thanks. I'll see you."

"There's more to life than seeing, John." She posed for him, in a more personal way than she did for customers, and John blushed. "You know how happy Ko Kim used to make Gus?" she asked. "Well, buy out my contract, and I can make you happy too. I've got half enough saved up, and you can have it."

"Mary—"

"That's a lot of money, John. I'm offering it to you."

"Mary, I'm fourteen years old."

"So what? I'm only a little older than that. You'd
want me if I wasn't one of Manley's whores."

"That's not true."

"Then you wouldn't want me?"

"Don't do that, please? You know I don't know how
to answer your questions."

"I'm just teasing, John. Friends can tease each other,
can't they?"

"Yes."

"Then you don't have to be mad at me like that."

"I'm sorry."

"Come up when you can, though, all right? I have
some new clothes to show you. And a book. I'm going
to read it."

"I will."

The flyer, an old military scouter from a war light-
years away, was parked nose-in against the back of the
brothel behind The Pit. Gus's handiwork was plain to
be seen. Three broad planks at the corner of the building were caved in, and the drainage pipe that John had
replaced only a week ago was crushed again. He
scratched his head and let out a long breath. He'd have
to come back later and settle with Manley about the
damage. Maybe it was time to drag the old man home,
whether he wanted to go or not. Before he spent all that
money. John regretted the last thought as soon as it was
formed. He didn't want that money. Either the fight had
been a setup for something he didn't want to do, or else
Cyclone Tom really was just a poor idiot. Either way,
he didn't want it. But then again the twins did need
things, and three hundred was three hundred. And
Ling-Ling might be needing Dr. Samuels, and he already owed the doctor twice that much, twice over.

Sometimes having money could be as troublesome as not having it.

His grandfather was a bigger problem than the money, though. Fifty days had passed since Ko Kim had suffered what he called her "outrage," and forty-nine had passed since Gus had lost his third wife, this time to suicide. No one had seen him sober since. That wasn't much of a change from when Ko Kim was healthy and Olina was alive, but back then at least Ko Kim had been able to keep the old man reasonably nourished and passably clean.

He realized that he'd forgotten to ask Gus for the keys to the flyer. If it weren't for Ling-Ling he'd take off running back home and leave the old scouter where it was. One of the things Ko Kim had taught him was that hard running burns hard anger. That was probably what she was doing right now, running. But he didn't think it was because of him. She'd heard every word said at The Pit, so she'd know it hadn't been his fault. No, it wasn't him she was angry about. It was probably the sickness.

John decided he wasn't going back to The Pit for Gus's keys. He hated that place, especially when they'd been swilling beer. On Gus's money this time, so it would go on all day and probably night.

Ho, Big John, I got a cow I bet you can't lift. Ho, Big John, my flyer's broken down. Will you carry it home for me? Ho, Big John, how big you gonna be when you're a real man?

He knew what they'd be talking about right now, Gus and his friends, and Iris. There would be talk, and bigger talk, and then someone would have an inspiration. Applause. More beer. A newly crowned genius. A few comments aimed carefully away from that Duelist, Tom, and right at Iris, and the comments would get louder and louder. Then Iris would get mad and reluctantly agree, as if the thought had never entered her mind. By noon it would be all over Dennis Town. Big John's going to fight that touring Duelist, Cyclone Tom.

Let's get some bets going!

Okay, but first nobody says a word about what happened to Wilfred Manley. Agreed?

Right! Not a word. We'll get some of Manley's money, for once.

Right.

No, John wasn't going back in there.

The keys weren't important anyway. John walked up to the flyer's door and eyed just the right spot under the access lock, and slammed his fist into it. The door popped open. A few seconds later he had the ignition casement open and took out the primary circuit board. Scratching a diagonal groove into the board was a familiar routine, and his mind drifted while his hands did the delicate work. Iris was just another user—setting him against that poor addled imbecile for the town's entertainment, counting on a Duelist's reflexes to win. She wasn't the first user he'd ever seen. When that type saw John, the first thing they thought of was, "fight." And then, so fast it might as well be part of the same word, "money." He should be used to it by now. But there was a ready-made hole in his insides where the anger showed up every time it happened, and the anger fit just perfectly.

What angered him the most, he supposed, was that he just might do it—if it would bring the money he needed. To fix things at home, to send the twins off to school somewhere away from Gus, to pay at least a big part of the family debts. To get Mary out of the brothel and let her go anywhere she wanted.

He wondered how long Cyclone Tom had been a credentialed Duelist. How high had he been ranked? Journeyman? Expert? Master? He must've been hurt badly, judging from the way he was now. Now that John thought about it he didn't think it was drugs, because drugs took the body along with the mind. Maybe Cyclone Tom had just tried to go on too long, with too little skill. And just enough sense to avoid death matches against healthy Duelists.

John decided that he pitied circus fighters. They were byproducts of a noble profession, reduced to fighting wild animals, local toughs—and giant freaks. But pitiable or not, that Tom had been a Duelist. No matter what happened this morning, that meant Tom's skills were on a level that no amateur could ever match. There was something magical about those Duel Schools that only their graduates knew. And they weren't talking, because the Duelist Union wasn't shy about sending assassins after anyone who gave out training secrets, or even appeared likely to.

Cyclone Tom might not deserve his pity, though. He could be a user, too, only pretending to be addled. John didn't think so, but it was possible.

But none of that made any difference: Iris didn't, or Cyclone Tom, or anything they might be trying to set up. No difference at all. That was because John knew what everyone from New Cardiff to Portside, and maybe everywhere else on Janus, knew. No one could whip Big John. Grown men, big ones, had tried ever since Gus set up his first fight at the age of ten. John always won. He had secrets, too. He knew how to make his opponents think he was only big and strong. He knew how to take a pounding all afternoon if he had to, and wait for the right moment to end it. He knew how to hit so hard he could drive his fist elbow-deep into a dead bull. He always won. That was just the way it was.

When the circuit board was etched out, he took a length of copper wire from the tool kit and pressed it into the groove. Perfect fit. He snapped the board back in place and the engine snorted to life. Then he got out of the flyer and pushed it back away from the building and out onto Mason Street. The street was empty, as usual. Plenty of room to take off.

He'd just cleared the rooftops of Dennis Town when he spotted the twins walking their horses into town on the east road. He banked to the east to intercept them. Glenda and Brenda were eleven years old, the products of Gus's second marriage. Technically they were John's aunts. The only way most people could tell them apart was the rose-colored birthmark, about the size of a thumb-print, in the center of Brenda's forehead. But sometimes they'd get into Ko Kim's cosmetics and switch things around.

John loved flying. It was quiet in the air, except for a strange engine noise he'd never been able to pin down and fix. It sounded like two birds fighting over a worm. That, and the doors always rattled because they weren't made for this particular flyer and never had fit right. The air always smelled, too. According to Gus this had been a hospital vehicle in that war somewhere out in the night sky. The smell was supposed to be from the dead people the flyer had carried, and from the little pieces of flesh that had been kicked under the seats and rotted there. John was used to those things, though, and they didn't enter his mind very often. It was the stillness he loved, being the only thing moving up there. Dennis Town wasn't very big to begin with. It looked even smaller from the air. This time of day there weren't many people out. Mostly it was just buildings, the tallest one three stories high, and empty streets laid out like the lines on the quilts Ko Kim used to make. To the north, on his left, was Farnham River. It wasn't much more than a trickle this time of year, down at the bottom of a riverbed that twisted north and south like a giant snake sleeping in the desert. The only times John had the chance to fly were when he was on the way to do something, or coming back from whatever work he could find. But while he was up there no one talked at him, or asked him any questions, or told him what he should be doing right then. "Solitude," Ko Kim used to say, "can be an unspeakable joy."

He landed the flyer thirty feet ahead of the twins and the horses, and eased the circuit board a few inches out to shut down the engine. For once Glenda and Brenda didn't try to run. They looked exhausted. In this heat, they'd probably walked all the way to spare the horses.

John popped the door open and jumped to the ground. "What are you two doing?" The twins had blue eyes and long hair the color of desert sand. Today they were wearing identical hats that covered their faces in shade.

"Not that we have to answer to you," Brenda said, "but any fool can see we were out riding."

John eyed the horses' hooves. They were covered with black powder. "You went by the augite mines again. Didn't Gus tell you two to stay away from there?"

"That's between Poppa and us," Glenda said.

"He's not coming home today," John told them. "He's got money." He saw the pain in their eyes, and softened his tone. "But I told him about Ling-Ling. Maybe he'll be along later."

"Sure he will." Brenda started walking and gave Rubin's reins a little tug. The old horse nodded its head and followed her. Behind them walked Glenda and Hershel. They were angling off from John, giving him a wide berth. It was a useless thing to do, because if he wanted to catch them he would. He'd proved more than once that he could run down the horses.

"Why don't you two take the flyer and go home?" John asked. "There's nothing you can do here. Gus will come home when he's ready."

"Poppa knows what he's doing," Glenda said. "We don't need you to tell us what Poppa's going to do."

John was trying to remember how Ko Kim handled them. That brought her picture to his mind, and as always the answer to his problem arrived with her. "Ling-Ling could have that foal any time now. What will she think if you're not there to help her?"

The twins exchanged a worried glance. Instant agreement flashed between them. Brenda said, "No keys, right?"

"That's right."

"Good," Glenda said. "It's more fun that way."

"Hershel and Rubin are tired," Brenda said. "With all four of us in the flyer, it won't take your weight."

"That's all right." Another mental picture of Ko Kim, this time running for home, settled in his mind.

"You four go ahead. But I think you should go straight home and check on Ling-Ling. And if you see Ko Kim on the way, don't fly down and frighten her. She doesn't think that's funny anymore."

"All right," they said together.

Rubin and Hershel were already nosing at the flyer's cargo door. Neither of them particularly liked flying, but they preferred it to walking in heat this bad. When the horses were aboard and the twins had moved up to the pilot's station, the craft flared to life and lifted off at a shallow angle, planing smoothly up to cruising altitude. That was for the horses, John knew. Normally the girls stood the flyer on its tail and screamed for the sky at full throttle. Almost immediately, the twins began a slow descent that would take them smoothly home.

Home was fourteen miles due west, on the other side of Dennis Town. John skirted the city at a moderate trot and then broke into a full-ahead run. He wouldn't slacken the pace until he reached the barn, behind the house. No one but Ko Kim had ever run this distance with him. It was never a race, although she always believed, or pretended to believe, that it was. If they were running together right now it would be her turn to win. But they hadn't run together since the outrage in Portside, fifty days before.

John had been ten years old the time Gus broke the bank at The Pit. Because the old man was blind drunk he accepted Ko Kim's brothel contract and a year's free drinking as payment from Wilfred Manley. When he sobered up a week or so later Gus told Ko Kim to go home, wherever that was. But she wouldn't leave him. His wife Olina wasn't doing much at the place by then,

so Gus took Ko Kim as a sort-of wife and told Olina
she could get the hell out and come back if she ever got
her sense of gratitude back. But Olina wouldn't leave
either. The twins didn't care either way, about either of
the women. As long as they had Gus to look after they
were happy. Somehow that jumble of personalities became a stable household.

John had been wary of Ko Kim at first, the way he
was wary of all strangers. But Ko Kim never looked at
him in *that way*, and never once made a joke about his
size. However she did find him, along with everything
else in life, hysterically funny. He asked her why.

"There are animals that can change color," she told
him, "even their odor and their size."

"My color and my odor are all right, I guess," John
said. "But it would be nice to be able to change other
things. Animals are lucky, those that can do that."

"But don't you see," Ko Kim explained, "human beings have something even better. We have minds. We
select a role to survive in, and that's where we live."

John didn't know what she meant, but it sounded
like something too important to interrupt with a question.

"Learn to act," Ko Kim told him. "And learn to be
absurd. It makes your friends laugh and your enemies
crazy. And it gives you something to hide the fear behind."

That, he understood. "I'm not afraid," he told her.
"Not of anything."

"I can see that you're very brave, Grandson John."

She was about twenty-five, and her calling him
"grandson" gave John a good idea of what she meant
by being absurd. They started laughing at the same

time, and finished together. "You're too young and I'm too big for me to be your grandson," he said.

"But you're far too handsome a man to be my friend," was Ko Kim's reply. "Grandfather Gus would be quite jealous. Will you be my brother?" So from then on she was Sister Kim. And he was Brother John.

But only to each other.

Sister Kim never did tell him how she came to work in a brothel. John knew what a brothel was, and that some people had to work there even when they didn't want to. But he sensed that asking would make her sad, so he never did. Everything else, they talked about. She told him about life in the Great Domain, eight hundred settled worlds now and still growing. She was from Politan, a newly terraformed world in the Jericho System. Her parents were dead, like his were. He couldn't remember why she'd told him that. But he remembered feeling better after she did. It was hard to remember a time when Sister Kim wasn't making him feel better, or laughing with him, about one thing or another. The little boy who lived in a giant's body loved her so hard, sometimes he sat up nights just thinking and smiling about it.

Maybe Gus loved her, too. He never said so. The old man cursed everybody, always, and so it was generally impossible to tell what he really felt about someone. Even his best friends had traded knife scars with him over the years. But he did give Ko Kim a home, and he never raised a hand against her. No matter how stinking drunk he was. With Sister Kim around the dusty old house always shone, and smelled of new flowers. Until the outrage.

Four years to the day after he brought her home, fifty days before John met Cyclone Tom, Gus sat down at one

of Wilfred Manley's card tables and did well enough to
cross the room and buy a pair of vacations at Portside,
eleven hundred miles away across the mountains. Trips
to Portside were one of the few things Gus became excited about. Ko Kim said he should take Olina. Olina
said she didn't want to go. Gus reminded Olina that
he'd never asked her to go, to begin with. And because
it wouldn't be fair, he said, to decide between Glenda
and Brenda, who begged to go with him, he told Ko Kim
to pack some clothes. Besides, there was a carnival in
town, and he said Ko Kim would be the best person to
show him what a carnival was like from the inside. That
was the only time John had ever seen her cry.

Two mornings later in Portside Ko Kim took a sun-
rise walk down to the carnival midway. Gus was sleeping at the hotel and never saw what happened. She was
attacked and beaten nearly to death. When the Peacekeepers found Ko Kim there was a tiny piece of tattooed
skin clenched in her left hand. Her silky black hair had
been hacked away, and her tongue had been cut out. So
had her right eye. The left one was punctured.

After a month she got some sight back through her
left eye, but it was so damaged that she still couldn't
see much of anything within fifty feet or so. The Peacekeeper lieutenant who put the report together had told
John that she'd have lost that eye too, but the way she
fought back must have made her attacker worry about
being marked up even more than having a patch of skin
ripped away. Whoever it was, therefore, was worried
about being easy to catch. The Peacekeeper seemed to
think that was a major clue.

But the worst part, the part the doctors said would
never heal and just keep getting worse, was her mind.

She'd been injected through the nasal opening with a virus that was eating her brain away. Except for the tattooed skin, that was the only clue they had to whoever attacked her. The virus had been used on two other worlds in the same Common Law group as Janus. There was a reason, the Peacekeeper said. If caught, the attacker couldn't be executed. Because strictly speaking, no murder had been committed. But in effect there was no witness left alive. Ko Kim was too damaged for a court to honor her testimony.

The day after Gus returned from Portside and told everyone what had happened, Olina hanged herself in the barn. That was how John found out that she loved Ko Kim, too.

So with his best friend and teacher gone, and with Gus committing suicide at a slower pace than Olina, John was the head of the family. He was fourteen, possibly the largest and strongest human being on Janus, and sometimes very frightened. But he'd learned something about taking a role and living in it. He knew about acting. So he never let it show.

John found Ko Kim sitting in the dirt about half a mile from the house. She was all right, she said with hand-signs. But she didn't know where she was going. Or who he was. He carried her home, and she slept all the way.

Just after midnight the trouble started. It started with each of the twins grabbing one of John's feet and trying to haul him out of bed.

"Ling-Ling had her foal!" Glenda said.

"It's a filly!" Brenda added.

John sat up and sighed. It figured. After putting Ko Kim to bed he'd sat up with the stubborn Ling-Ling until she'd stopped moaning and fallen asleep. Then he'd gone off to bed, and she'd done all the work herself. And of course the twins had sensed the moment and gone to her. Sometimes he worked too hard, for nothing.

"Well, are you coming, or not?" That was Glenda.

They were almost to the barn when the eastern sky came alive with lights and sirens. John saw three flyers at first, and then two more cut their lights on. One aimed a searchlight down at the house. They circled at about sixty feet. From the barn came the startled snuffling of the two stallions, and a terrified cry from Ling-Ling.

John turned to the twins and shouted above the noise, "Get back to the house and get the Barrow rifle out. Stay there, both of you."

"But Ling-Ling!"

"Go!"

Brenda and Glenda bolted for the house. The flyer with the searchlight landed twenty feet in front of John. The other four circled again, then came down at thirty-foot intervals in a half-circle behind the first. The precision of their maneuvering told John they weren't Gus's friends bringing him back from the party. He knew, then, who it had to be.

"Ho, Big John!"

Wilfred Manley himself stepped out of the flyer.

"Ho, Mr. Manley. I'd appreciate it if you'd shut down that big light and those sirens."

"Sure, Big John." He raised an arm, then dropped it. The searchlight went black and the sirens stopped. All that was left were the landing lights, crisscrossing the field with bands of brightness and long, stark shadows from the vehicles.

Manley approached the youth and extended a hand. He was smiling. He was a neat and compact man with a shock of thick brown hair that reached nearly to his right shoulder. He was close to a hundred, ten years or so older than Gus. But he looked about half that age. Where Gus was an old man in every sense of the word, Wilfred Manley was only old if years alone counted. He owned The Pit—the bar, the brothel, the casino, all of it—along with farms, the water treatment plant, and the closed augite mines around Dennis Town.

John shook the offered hand. "What can I do for you, Mr. Manley?" He could sense the rifles trained on him from the other flyers.

"Call me Wilfred, Big John. How long have I been telling you to call me Wilfred?"

"Since you first asked me to come work for you, about a year ago."

"It was a good offer, John. You should have taken it."

"Sir, is this about Gus? Because whatever money he had, that's all we've got right now. I'll have to work off the damage to that wall, and whatever else he owes."

Manley ignored the question and looked toward the barn. "I understand Ling-Ling was due. Did she have that foal yet?"

"Yes, sir, a filly. I was on my way to see it."

"Wonderful! I'm always interested in new stock." He grinned up at John. "And how are those two little aunts of yours?"

John's hands clenched into fists. "What is it you want, Mr. Manley?"

"Oh, this is just a courtesy call." His grin became broader. "If I know those two girls, one of them's got your Barrow aimed at my head right this moment. Do you think they'll shoot?"

"Not without reason, sir. And if they hear you asking about them again, that will be reason enough."

Manley's smile disappeared. "I came to show you this." He unfolded a document from his pocket and passed it to John. "Keep it. It's a copy."

The print was too small to read in the lights from the flyers.

"I'll save you the trouble," Manley said. "That's a wagering chit, signed and legally witnessed. The bet is that you will defeat in single combat one Thomas Klaus Herdtmacher, graduate of Barrow Duelist Academy, said combat to take place three nights from this date. If you win, your grandfather will receive a cash payment equaling ten times the assessed market value of this property, and everything on it. If you lose, said property and all legal authority your grandfather now maintains will transfer to the holder of that note." The small man paused to allow his emphasis to sink in. "And said holder of said note happens to be one Wilfred Aaron Manley."

John crumpled the paper and dropped it to the dirt. "This is worthless," he said tightly. "If he lost money at your casino, that's one thing. But this is about something that hasn't happened yet. That makes it a regular contract, which is meaningless because Gus was drunk when he signed it. He's always drunk, and everybody knows it. And anyway, I'm past thirteen now. So I'm not his ward and I'm not bound by anything he signs. Even if it is legal, and I don't think it is."

Manly gave the sneer he reserved for big casino winners. "You've been listening to Dr. Samuels again. Listen, boy. Gus was drunk when he signed a contract to accept Ko Kim from me. That was something that hadn't happened yet, wasn't it? And I honored that contract, didn't I? The whole town laughed at me. At me!"

"It was just funny, Mr. Manley. Nobody meant anything by it."

"I could've kept that whore and not owed him anything, because Gus couldn't even remember being there that night. But I honored his signature on that contract. I delivered Ko Kim, just as I promised. That's called precedent, boy, acceptable in any court."

"That still doesn't bind me to fight that Duelist."

"That's true, Big John. You're not bound by anything he signs. I don't dispute that at all. But your aunts are. Glenda and Brenda will become my legal wards if you don't win the fight your grandfather agreed to."

John had taken a half-step forward before he stopped himself. Manley jumped back and raised his arm again. "I close my fist and you're dead, boy."

"We both are, Mr. Manley."

Manley lowered his arm. "A stand-off, then." He smiled again, this time with his eyes, too. "Exciting, isn't it? I love little times like this. Death so close and everything, but not close enough to touch." He was quiet for a few seconds. "The fight's three nights from tonight. The time and place are on that chit. Read it. If you're a minute late, your grandfather forfeits." And then, "Death and me, you and me. Close but you can't touch me. Neither one can."

John watched him turn and climb back into the flyer. Just before he shut the door, there was a woman's laughter. It sounded like Iris.

As the flyers lifted off in formation, something thudded to the ground. Manley's searchlight illuminated what they'd dropped, then swung to catch John in the eyes. The sirens switched on again and the flyers circled the house once. They flew low over John, in line like a twisting snake, then streaked eastward toward Dennis Town.

Gus was still breathing, but his mouth was caked with blood and he smelled like an open sewer. His arms and legs were broken.

"Poppa!" Glenda and Brenda screamed in one voice as they ran from the house.

"Get the flyer," John said. "We're going to have to wake Dr. Samuels up."

John had never seen the twins as cheerful as they were the next morning. He woke from a fitful sleep to find them both jumping on his bed, still dripping from their bath, pounding his head with pillows.

"What?" The memory of what had happened came back all at once. He sat up groggily and rubbed his face. The twins threw themselves at him, kissed him, and ran giggling from the room.

The bathwater was still warm. By the time he was shaved and dressed they had breakfast ready, the first meal they'd cooked in months, and were in their best clothes. Brenda met him at the kitchen door and latched on to his hand, tugging him toward the table. "Eat while it's hot," she said. "Then we'll go see Poppa."

"Just a minute," John said. He passed through the kitchen and Olina's old room, to look in on Ko Kim. Sometime during the night she had awakened and changed into her sleeping shirt. A good sign, he thought. She knew where she was and where her things were. He'd hoped to be able to talk with her about everything that was going on, as he had with Dr. Samuels. The physician had had an interesting idea. He wanted to hear what Ko Kim thought about it. Instead he left her sleeping, and went back to the kitchen.

"Well?" Glenda asked.

"She looks good," John said.

"What are you talking about?"

"Ko Kim, I think," Brenda said.

Glenda released a long, slow breath. "John, will you stop wasting time and eat? We have to go."

On the table were pancakes, sausages, slices of beef, fried mayos, boiled onions, and beans. It was a week's worth of food.

"Just take a little," Brenda said. "We're taking the rest to Poppa."

While he ate, the twins kept up a steady stream of chatter. Glenda asked, "Did Bill say when Poppa could come home?"

"He's Dr. Samuels, Glenda. And no, he didn't. I'd guess a few days. There was some internal bleeding."

"But he's all right."

"Yes."

"That's what matters, he's all right. And he can't get in any trouble at Bill's—Dr. Samuels' house. And then he'll have to stay here, at least until his bones are healed."

"And," Brenda said, with the biggest smile John had

ever seen on her face, "we're going to be rich." The
twins looked at each other, and broke out laughing.

John had told them what Gus had done, on the ride
home from the doctor's house. He expected anger,
maybe panic, and he had a little speech ready to calm
them down. He began by telling them that he'd already
fought this Duelist and beaten him. They weren't listening. The twins were both caught up in instant, un-
bounded joy. Ten times what the house was worth, and
everything Gus owned! It never occurred to either of
them that John could lose. He was their nephew, the
strong boy, the unbeatable horse in an easy race. Gus
was the mastermind. Poppa was the genius who had
lured Wilfred Manley into making a sure-lose bet.

But John knew it wasn't that simple. That was what
he'd hoped to talk with Ko Kim about. Dr. Samuels
was a smart man and his idea sounded good. But Ko
Kim was smarter when it came to people.

The twins began packing the food into boxes, leaving John what was already on his plate. "Everything
was good?" Brenda asked.

"Gus will be proud of you," John said.

She kissed his cheek again. "Do you want to go with
us? You can drive."

"Someone should stay and look after Ling-Ling," he
said. The mare was in perfect condition, he knew, or the
twins would be out in the barn with her. But during the
night he'd come to a few conclusions. One of them was
that the twins would be safer, well clear of him. "You
two go ahead. But don't be disappointed if Gus isn't
conscious yet."

"That doesn't matter," Glenda said.

"You know," John said as he'd planned to say, "Dr.

Samuels might appreciate your help for a day or two. Gus can be a hard man to take care of."

"We already thought of that," Glenda said. "Why do you think we made all this food? And don't you say anything about Gus, is that all right? You're always saying things about him."

"That's right," Brenda said. "It's Poppa who got hurt, and it's Poppa who's making us rich. So you better watch what you say."

"Just remember," John said, "you'll be guests."

Without another word or another look at John, they finished gathering the food and stamped out the door. As he was emptying his plate he heard the flyer come to life. He stood at the kitchen window and watched it rock back on its tail and go screaming for the sky. A few seconds later he saw another flyer rise up from behind a line of trees a mile away. It followed the twins toward Dennis Town.

Good, John thought. That meant that at least part of what he'd figured out was right. That, in turn, gave him confidence about going ahead with Dr. Samuels' plan.

He went back to Ko Kim's room and sat down on the floor, watching her sleep. With her eyes closed, in the soft morning light, her scars couldn't be seen. At those times she still had the prettiest face he'd ever seen. And her hair wasn't so shaggy anymore. But it was still a long way from being the liquid blackness that used to pour over her shoulders and halfway down her back.

"Here's what I think," John said quietly. "Manley's seen me fight a dozen times or more. He knows what I can do. And he knows what happened between me and his Duelist. But he made the bet anyway. And he gave ten-to-one odds. That means what happened was a

setup, like I thought it might be. But I don't think it
started yesterday, Sister Kim. He probably brought Iris
and that circus-fighter to Dennis Town. That would be
to get revenge on Gus, and to add the twins to his
brothel. It wouldn't take much to make Gus sign that
betting chit. Some whiskey and some big talk about
how next time, Cyclone Tom . . . his real name is
Herdtmacher, it says so on Manley's paper . . . how
he's going to hurt me bad. Maybe Gus wouldn't sign at
first, and that's why the ten-to-one odds. And he made
it three nights from tonight, to give the other bets some
time to grow. That means Manley is betting most of
what he owns, if not all of it. And that means when this
is over either he'll be ruined or he'll own everything in
Dennis Town that's worth owning. And that means he's
sure he's going to win."

Ko Kim coughed and moved her head on the pillow.
John didn't plan to wake her up. Since the outrage had
happened she'd been hard to wake up. But if she came
around, that would be all right. She'd know what he
should do. He'd just have to remember to look away
when she opened her eyes. That was for his sake, not
hers; she couldn't see his expression when he was this
close.

"So," he continued, "how can he be so sure? What
happened between me and his Duelist wasn't really a
fight, but I took his measure. Remember what you
taught me about acting? You said some people are so
good at it, you never suspect. But no one is good
enough to fake that look that was in his eyes when I hit
him. I surprised him, Sister Kim. And I hurt him. That
means I can beat him. I know it won't be easy again.
It'll probably be the hardest fight I've ever had. But he

can pound on me all night, he can throw kicks and punches I never thought of, and it won't matter. I can beat him. All I have to do is surprise him one good time and it'll be over.

"So how can Manley be so sure? Well, there's forfeit. If I don't fight, Gus forfeits. But then all the other bets would be off, and Manley wouldn't get a thing from them. So he won't have me killed or taken off somewhere. And he won't threaten the twins because if he uses that to force me to lose, word will get out. The folks in Dennis town would kill Manley and me, both of us. So he'll make sure nothing happens to Glenda and Brenda, because if it does everyone will believe he did it. He's having them followed right now, just for that reason.

John leaned closer to Ko Kim. "So here's what he's going to do. He's going to make sure I show up for the fight, and that I try the best I can. But he doesn't want me healthy. He thinks Cyclone Tom can win this time, but you know how Manley is. Just to be sure, something's going to happen to me right before the fight. Not too soon before, because then the town could ask the Council to put the fight off until I'm better. It'll happen right before, like I said. But you see, Sister Kim, I'm not going to be there. For five or six hours, no one's going to know where I am. Then half a minute before the fight has to start, I'll show up. And I'll win."

He straightened and added, "There's more I could tell you. But I've got some things to do, and somewhere to go. So, what do you think, Sister Kim?"

It was then, when he sat back with the warm assurance he'd always felt when she was proud of him, that Ko Kim woke up. Her eyelids flicked open and John

saw the gelled pit on one side and the swollen streaks
of red on the other. She opened her mouth to its widest
and screamed. It was a hollow, scratchy sound welling
up from her damaged throat and modulated by the
stump that had been her tongue.

John jumped to his feet and ran from the room, in
terror. He was outside and past the barn before he
stopped running. Bending so that his hands were on his
knees, he gulped air like a bellows. What is wrong with
you! his mind screamed at him. That's Sister Kim!
She's hurt and sick, and she needs you. She is Sister
Kim!

When he entered her room again, Ko Kim was lying
on her back. Her eyelids and mouth were still open. Her
breath came in short gasps.

"Sister Kim?" he said. When there was no response
he repeated her name several times, gently shaking her
shoulder. Her feet began twitching, as if she were trying to run. John sat on the floor next to the bed and put
his massive hand over hers. "Dr. Samuels said this is
how it will be when you're not going to wake up anymore. He said there's nothing anyone can do. But you
and I don't believe that, do we? You go ahead and
sleep, Sister Kim. Like I told you, I've got some things
to do, and then somewhere to go. And I'm taking you
with me, all right? You just rest, and I'll be back. Then
we'll go somewhere together."

John spent the next few hours repairing the corral
behind the barn. After a quick lunch he piled oats and
hay in the fenced-off area and opened the barn's back
door for Ling-Ling. Then he shooed the stallions out
the front door and locked it. Rubin and Hershel could
forage for themselves while he was gone.

He checked again on Ko Kim. She was lying on her side now, the way she normally slept. John thought that was a good sign. But he still planned to take her with him when he got back from Dennis Town.

He left the house and took off running. It was easy to imagine Ko Kim beside him as the miles passed behind him. Halfway to Dennis Town he saw a flyer approaching from the east, flying low to the ground. He was surprised it had taken Manley so long to check on him. His imaginary running companion started laughing. He knew what she was thinking. ". . . it will make your enemies crazy." This was a good time for a little absurdity.

He waited until he spotted a shallow depression ahead, then shortened his stride and began scuffing his feet hard against the loose dirt. A cloud of dust began forming behind him. When it was rising thick and high, he stopped abruptly and ran a few paces back. He lay down in the depression and covered himself with sand and scrub brush. By the time the dust settled down again John had effectively disappeared from sight. This was a trick Ko Kim had showed him years before. More than once they had lain hidden, giggling like children while Gus flew over them.

The flyer made several low passes, kicking up more dust, before it finally banked and streaked off toward town. John stood up and brushed himself off. "He's got the radio going about now, Sister Kim," he said, laughing. "Think about what he's saying to Manley. How can he explain losing someone as big as me, when there's nothing out here to hide behind? I have a feeling he's going to be looking for a job in another town."

John was three miles outside of Dennis Town, run-

ning at full speed, when three more flyers approached
him at low altitude and maneuvered into formation behind him. "Here we go," he said aloud. "Time to pick a
role and live in it for a while. You won't like this one,
though. I'm sorry." He felt himself leaving Ko Kim behind, along with the person he had been for fourteen
years. "I'll be back for you," he said. It was easy then
to slip into a new persona, one he'd only dreamed of
before.

Wilfred Manley's offices occupied the second floor of
a building directly across Carney Street from The
Pit. The first floor was living quarters for the men who
carried out his orders and saw to it that the residents of
Dennis Town and outlying areas obeyed Manley's
rules. John didn't wait for the door to be answered.
After knocking once he pushed it open and walked inside. He entered a large room, semidark, with chairs,
couches, and small tables just about everywhere on the
floor. A wide crack in the ceiling ran from one corner
to the opposite side. At the far end of the room was a
staircase leading to Manley's private suite. Five men
jumped up from their seats.

"Keep out of my way," John said. After that he ignored them. No one tried to intercept him before he
reached the stairs.

As he climbed the last two steps he heard a buzzer
sounding from behind the door to his right. He knocked
once and was about to kick it in when the door opened.
A tall man with short red hair stood there. "What do
you want?" he asked. "If you need to see Mr. Manley

you can make an app—" John shoved him aside and walked in.

This was another large room, but brightly lit. It was cluttered with overstuffed furniture in every imaginable shade of green and blue. The temperature was about twenty degrees cooler than the heat downstairs and outside. To John's left Wilfred Manley was sitting behind a polished wooden desk. He wore a relaxed smile. "It's all right, Dexter," he said. "My friend John is always welcome here."

John took a minute to look around at the walls. The one behind Manley bore variously sized metal bars mounted like museum exhibits. They were all different colors, and each one was polished to a shine that made the bars glow with an aura that seemed almost alive. This effect was the result of using augite, the mineral that came from the mines owned by Wilfred Manley. The bars were beautiful to look at. The problem was that the luster on the metal had never been functional. It was merely stylish, and the style had begun losing favor thirty years ago. A few orders still came in, just enough to keep a few people working. But commerce in the mineral wasn't enough to support the town anymore. Wilfred Manley continued to insist that augite would be in demand again, more than ever before. Some of the people in Dennis Town still listened to him.

The other three walls were covered with framed works of art, or what Manley considered to be art. They ranged from pristine portraits to obscene holo-images. John had heard about this. These were depictions of the best of Manley's "stock," his male and female whores, dating back more than fifty years since he'd opened the bordello. The portrait of Ko Kim was modest and almost as beautiful as she herself had been. But to John's mind having it in this room was an obscenity.

While John was looking at the walls, the five men from the first floor entered the room through a far door and separated. All five wore holstered Barrow pistols. Two of them took up positions on either side of Manley. The other three, and Dexter, stood to John's right. As the intruder approached Manley's desk they followed behind him at a distance calculated to be out of the giant's reach.

"I'm going to Portside," John said. "Get one of your flyers ready for me."

"Portside?" Manley sat up straight, then slumped back again. "Well, if you were planning to run from the fight I don't guess you'd be here to say so."

"You'll get your fight," John said. "I want that flyer ready in ten minutes."

"I'd be happy to rent you one," Manley said. "But there's the matter of money. Have you got any?" The two men flanking his chair grinned, along with their boss. Each of them had a hand resting on the Barrow pistol at his side. John assumed that at least one of the men behind him had a weapon pointed at his back.

"I don't plan to pay," John said. He didn't feel comfortable about this, even though he knew it was the best way to act. But a quick glance at Ko Kim's portrait made it easier. "I also want a driver who'll take me anywhere I say," he went on. "Along with an escort, and money for a night's room and food. I want all of that right now, Willie Boy."

Neither Manley nor his men were grinning now.

"Who the hell," Manley ground out between clenched teeth, "do you think you are?"

"You know who I am, Willie," John said. "I'm the man you expect to use to get even richer than you are. Right now I'm going to Portside. You pay for the trip and give me what I want, or I go alone. That means no one follows me. Anyone who tries, I'll break him in half. That means you lose sight of your investment. The only way you can stop me from going is to kill me. And that wouldn't help your plans at all, would it, Willie? All those people who bet on me, they'd kill you." He glared down at Manley and gave him a mocking smile. "So you aren't going to try to stop me, little man. And you're not going to send anyone after me unless I say it's all right. You're an ass, but you're not stupid. Besides, we've already seen how good your morons are at keeping track of me."

An angry voice came from behind him. "That was me, you freak."

"Milson, don't shoot him!" Manley screamed.

John turned to see the man reverse the Barrow in his hand and raise it like a club. Before the man had taken a full step, John had one hand around Milson's throat. With his other hand he gripped the man's wrist and twisted until it snapped. The pistol dropped to the floor. Milson struggled violently against the giant's grip.

"Open the window," John said.

"What?"

"Never mind." He lifted Milson, holding him out at arm's length. He spun a half step and released him. Milson flew eight feet through the air and crashed against the closed window. He slid to the floor, pulling the curtains with him.

"That glassite's pretty strong," John said, crossing the room after the unconscious man. "Once more ought to do it, though."

"That's enough!" Manley said tightly. He stood and opened a desk drawer.

"Did you want something, Willie?" John asked.

"Here," Manley said. He took out a set of keys and a money card. "These two will go with you," he said, pointing at Dexter and the man to his left. They were the largest of the six. "And I'll have three more following you. I almost hope you do try to run, Big John."

"No you don't, Little Willie," John said. "But don't cry. I'm coming back."

"Boy," Manley said, "in three days you're going to be dead. Your aunts are going to be the most used whores this place has ever seen. So have your fun now. Go ahead. But—" He turned ash white when a big fist stopped a fraction of an inch from his face.

John smiled down at him and dropped his arm. Manley sagged backward into his chair. "And I'm taking this with me," John said. He crossed to the wall and took down the portrait of Ko Kim. "And this one," he said, spotting one of his friend Mary.

"Here." He handed the portraits to Dexter. "If you drop these . . . well, just don't." To the other man Manley had chosen he said, "What's your name?"

"Lars," the man said. He was bald, with a thin black mustache beneath a bulbous nose.

"Lars," John said, "get the keys and the money card. Show me where my flyer is."

Without another glance at Manley he turned and walked back to the stairs. Dexter and Lars followed a few seconds later. As he reached the bottom of the staircase he heard Manley cursing and kicking the un-conscious figure on his floor.

"We can give her a new eye," the doctor said, "and the other one will heal itself, eventually. But John, there will never be anything in those eyes again. The woman you knew is gone." The doctor had a soft voice that matched her face perfectly.

"Dr. Samuels back in Dennis Town told me this would happen," John said. "I accept that, Doctor. But I don't believe the time is here yet."

Dr. Irene Mays stood up from her desk and crossed the small office to stand beside John. He was seated, bringing their eyes to the same level. "Anything that can be done, will be done," she said. "But you'll have to leave her here in the hospital. Can you do that, John?"

"You said she can't eat by herself, or . . . or anything she has to do."

"Not anymore."

"Did I wait too long?"

"John, what you did was the best thing anyone could have done for Ko Kim. You kept her at home where she was loved, and where she could hear familiar voices. I have no doubt that that helped to preserve her mind longer than if she'd been here since the attack. But now this is the best place she can be."

"There's nothing you can do about the virus." It wasn't a question.

"Nothing. Anything we might use to retard its growth or eliminate it would bear directly on the brain tissue it's living in. That would only hasten the inevitable result."

"I'll do what you think is best," John said. "For now, anyway." He stood and shook her offered hand. "Thank you, Dr. Mays. I'll make some arrangements with the administrator."

"Good luck, John."

He left her office and walked three doors down the hallway to another one. Dexter and Lars followed silently, as they had before, and waited outside. Half an hour later they followed him down to a large ward and stood in the doorway while he walked to a bed at the far end. John remained there for about ten minutes. When he left, Ko Kim had a fresh rose clutched in her left hand. She bore the same facial expression she'd worn since he'd returned to the house and carried her outside to the waiting flyer. The only difference was that now a white bandage covered her eyes.

His escort was hard-pressed to keep up with John as he traversed seven miles of walkways through the busy city of Portside. More than once a crowd formed between the escorts and John. If it weren't for the fact that he stood head and shoulders over the tallest people in the crowds, they'd have lost sight of him. The crowds gawked at the giant but moved out of his way when he showed no sign of slowing down.

He stopped only once, to ask final directions from a Peacekeeper. The uniformed man pointed to a ten-story building across the street and a block away.

The woman he wanted to see was in her office on the eighth floor. Lars and Dexter sat down gratefully in the hall while John went inside.

"Hello," he said as he entered the office and shut the door behind him. "Do you remember me?"

The woman looked up and drew a sharp breath. "Who could forget?"

That night at the hotel John ate more than he had ever put down in one sitting. The maitre d' accompanied the fifth serving and politely asked to see his money card. He gestured toward Lars, sitting with Dexter two tables away. Lars produced the card and sat down again. Then he stood and walked over to John.

"What do you want?" John asked.

"Dexter and me are hungry," Lars said timidly. "If you were to force us, we'd have to eat something. That would add to Manley's expense."

"Do it," John said.

"Thank you, sir." Lars walked back to his table, flashing a thumbs-up at Dexter.

The maitre d' was smiling when he returned with the money card. John accepted it and put it in his pocket. "Good enough?" he asked.

"Excellent, sir. Most excellent."

"Then do it all again," he said. His hands indicated the piles of empty plates in front of him. "And put everyone's meal on my account. Oh, and add fifty percent for you and your staff."

"Thank you, sir."

As the evening wore on most of the diners stopped by to thank him before they left. Most of them knew who he was. There couldn't be more than one on Janus of that size and age. A few of them asked for his signature as a souvenir. It was a strange sensation, answering polite questions from people who seemed to be in awe of him. And watching their eyes shine when he put his signature on whatever they handed him. He liked it.

Shortly before midnight the woman from the eighth-floor office entered the restaurant. She was accompanied by a sickly looking old man who gaped openly when John stood to shake hands. From a briefcase he produced two documents. John scanned them both quickly, then folded and tucked them in a pocket. He passed the woman Manley's money card. The two of them left and returned ten minutes later. They shook hands again, while the woman palmed the card and slipped it back to John.

"You two can stay for a meal," he offered. "And a couple of rooms for the night. Or a week, if you want."

"Thank you," the sickly looking man said. "But no. I am well compensated for being out at this awful hour. However, there is only so much one can take. But thank you."

"What about you, ma'am?" Dexter called out.

"You can stay with us," Lars added.

"I'm going home," she said, taking a step backward.

John turned around and glared at Manley's thugs. His expression put an end to their smiles. And to the truce they'd had for a while, he decided. He escorted the woman and the old man down to the street and thanked them again.

When they'd gone he said to Dexter, following ten feet behind him, "I'm going to my room. You two can sleep in the hall or in the flyer."

"What about Mr. Manley's money card?" Lars asked. "I'm supposed to keep it with me."

John threw it to him. "Get a room if you want to," he said. "But this time I didn't force you."

The next morning Lars and Dexter switched places with the three others Manley had sent. The two flyers took off together and headed for Dennis Town.

The man driving John's flyer was the youngest of the five, twenty or so. "I heard you bought Dexter and Lars a good meal," he said. "Maybe you're not as bad as Mr. Manley says. My name is—"

"I don't want to know your name," John said from the seat next to him. "I haven't decided if I'm going to kill you three, or not."

"What?"

"What I do want, is for you to tell me who did the work on Gus. Was it you?"

"No! I don't break old men's bones."

"Then who did?"

One of the men in the seat behind them said, "You don't have to tell him anything, Noddy." John turned around and looked at them for a full minute. Neither of the men said a word to the implied challenge, but stared back hard. Soon they both lowered their eyes. They looked enough alike to be brothers; large, dark, and muscular.

"All right," John said. "Then you tell me."

"Listen," the one to John's left said, "I don't think you're a bad sort either. But we still work for Wilfred Manley."

"And what do you suppose Willie would do if you told me what I want to know?"

Noddy barked out a short laugh. "He'd throw another fit, is what. That always tickles me. Why don't we tell him, Wolf?"

The other of the two men glared at his back. "Noddy, shut the hell up!"

"Why not tell him?" his apparent brother asked. "Like I said, we work for Wilfred Manley. We don't work for that witch. And I'm not afraid of her, are you?"

"You mean Iris," John said. He was thinking as fast as he could. "You're not answering my question. I already know about Iris. What I'm asking is, who did she get to beat him like that? Was it that Duelist I'm going to fight?"

"Tell him if you want to, Keeler," the one named Wolf said. "He's not listening to me."

"Wolf told you already," Keeler said. "Iris did it herself. You saw it, right, Noddy?"

"It was the ugliest thing I ever saw," the pilot said. "The old man was already passed out. She went on kicking him. And clubbing him with that pipe."

"So you stood there watching it happen," John said.

"No, I said something. I said if she kept on like that she was going to kill him. That got Manley worried. He told her she'd better stop because if Gus died, we'd have to shoot you down to stop you from coming after them. Then there wouldn't be any fight."

"He was right," John said. "The time to shoot me down is after the fight's over."

"Why would we do that?" Wolf asked innocently.

John knew, or believed, that Manley intended to have him attacked just before the fight started. They'd probably stun him and give him some kind of drug to slow his reflexes or blur his vision. But win or lose, they wouldn't let him live. Manley would kill him. It was insulting, that they assumed he hadn't figured out that much. He said angrily, "If I lose, Manley will have to kill me before he can get to my aunts. If I win he'll kill me for revenge."

All three of Manley's men broke out in laughter. "No offense, boy," Wolf said, "but you don't have a chance of winning. Not one chance in ten billion billion."

"He's right, John," Keeler said. "You're about the strongest and fastest person I've ever seen. But you're going up against a Duelist."

Wolf nodded his head solemnly. "He's a Grade One Expert," he said. "There's only about two hundred of them in the whole Great Domain."

"Only a Master Duelist ranks higher," Noddy said. "And there's about forty of them, I think. That's forty, out of what, about eight hundred billion people or so? Thomas Herdtmacher made his rank in only fifteen years after he graduated from Barrow Academy. That's a miracle, if you know anything about Duelists. And I do. He's light-years ahead of you, John. They say he can kill you, or mean anybody, in his—"

"I know," John said. "In his sleep." He shook his head sadly. He was amazed that the circus-fighter had once been ranked that highly. It was a long way to fall. As he'd explained to Sister Kim, he knew more about this Cyclone Tom than anyone else did. Herdtmacher could fool other people, and he had no doubt that the Duelist had been ordered not to try very hard at their first meeting. But John had seen his eyes at the one moment of their altercation that really mattered. He knew.

What these men were saying only convinced John that they didn't know very much about Manley's plans. That wasn't much of a surprise, when he thought about it. But they knew who'd beaten Gus almost to death. And now he knew. "You can drop me off at my house," he said. "If you're going to stay and keep an eye on me, you're going to work. And you'll bring your own food from town."

Noddy shook his head. "We know you're not going anywhere, John. You'll do what's right for your family. At least, you'll try. Manley's just scared. He's scared to death that Iris will make good on her threat if there's no fight. She gets half the winnings, you know."

That was interesting, John thought. "Willie's afraid of that woman? What did she threaten to do, pull out his pretty hair?"

"Like I said, I'm not afraid of her," Wolf said from the rear seat. "But she's a bad one. She told him she'd cut out his eyes and tongue."

"Manley says she's done it before," Keeler said. "She likes it."

John stared straight ahead and felt the blood pounding in his face. It took every bit of self-control he had to keep the rage from his voice. "I see," he said.

He watched the two flyers head for Dennis Town and went to check on the horses. One of the stallions, Hershel, he thought, had kicked in the front door to the barn. Both of them were standing asleep in their stalls, bellies bloated and snoring contentedly. Ling-Ling was pacing the corral. Just behind her was the bandy-legged foal. John scratched the mare's ears and spoke gently to her while the foal edged up against his leg. There was already a tiny white diamond patch on her throatlatch. So the sire had been Hershel, as he'd suspected. The foal smelled clean and she was dry. John climbed up to the loft and tossed out more hay and oats. Then he filled the trough with fresh water and went inside the house.

A stranger was sitting at the kitchen table when John entered. He stopped in midstride. "Who are you? What are you doing in my house?" He waited for an answer. When none came he strode past the stranger and checked the rest of the house. It was empty. Nothing appeared to have been disturbed. He went back to the kitchen. The stranger hadn't moved. "Well?"

The man looked up at him with gray, impassive eyes. His gaze went from John's face down his body, then up again, pausing on the chest and shoulders of the boy giant. His expression never changed. At last he looked into John's eyes and focused there. It seemed he was expecting something. The effect was strange and annoying. As though John were horseflesh being sold at auction.

"Mister," John said, "you'd better tell me who you are and what you're doing here." The stranger was of medium height, slightly under six feet. John estimated his weight at about two hundred pounds. He had heavy arms and a broad chest, and was clean-shaven. His hair was done in tight little ringlets, dusty brown with streaks of gray in it. Probably about fifty, John thought. The twins would call him horse-faced and mean it as a compliment; the bridge of his nose was unusually long and straight. He was wearing a tunic that was plain, in a deep blue color.

John allowed a minute to pass before he spoke again. "If you can't talk, then nod. Do you want something? Are you hungry?"

The man still gazed at him, revealing nothing. After another minute had passed John stood over the seated man. "Outside, then," he said. The boy reached down and lifted the man by the front of his tunic. He offered no resistance, and kept the same impassive look on his face. John carried him dangling at arm's length out the door.

He· dropped him about a hundred feet from the house. The man reached for a tunic pocket. "What is that?" John lunged for the hand but the man turned away just enough to make him miss. He drew out a red cloth-wrapped object and held it out to John. It looked like a scroll.

"Take," he said. "Unwrap." The man's voice was deep and gravelly. What he'd said was accented in a way John had never heard before.

John opened the bundle. He expected some kind of legal proclamation. Harassment, from Wilfred Manley. But it was a work of art: a long and ornate silver dagger. Next to it was a shorter package, also wrapped in the red cloth.

"Unwrap also," the man said.

This was a sheath for the dagger. It was wet with what looked like yellow ink. John looked at the man and saw that he was watching him as he had before. Like he expected something. After a few seconds he thought he knew what the man wanted him to do. He slid the sheath over the gleaming dagger blade, using the cloth to keep his hands clean.

The man nodded. "Now," he said. "Mark you me."

"What?"

"Mark. Hit. With weapon, me."

John stared at him. "Mister, what is this about? Are

you a friend of Cyclone Tom? Thomas Herdtmacher?
Another Duelist trying to scare me?"

"Duelist, yes," the man said. "Yes, I am he. Thomas
Klaus Herdtmacher. You are Herr Chon. You are fighter
for me, yes?"

The air went thick and hard to breathe. "You're . . .
you're Herdtmacher?"

"I am Thomas Klaus Herdtmacher," the man repeated. "Herr Manley sass daggers. So I must know
first that you are competent. *Verstehen?* Understand?"

"Knives? And you're . . . not Cyclone Tom." It all fit
together now. No wonder those three on the flyer were
so positive he'd lose. And no wonder they laughed one
minute and seemed to feel sorry for him the next.
They'd known what he was thinking. Everyone who'd
be betting on him was thinking the same thing he had.
They'd all assumed that Cyclone Tom and Thomas
Herdtmacher were the same man. But as John pondered
this development he realized that no one had claimed,
directly, that they were one and the same. The wagering chit spelled out who he had to fight. Legally and
exactly. Manley had even advised him, in front of wit-
nesses, to read it.

He stared at Thomas Klaus Herdtmacher, Grade One
Expert Duelist. One of only two hundred out of eight
hundred billion people. Not a circus fighter. Not an ex-
anything. A Grade One Expert, in his prime. Like a
cave-in at the mines it hit him all at once. He knew
what this meant to the future of his family. Manley—or
Iris—had set it up beautifully. And if Herdtmacher
hadn't come to his house, he'd never have known until
he showed up, as he planned, thirty seconds before the
fight.

Herdtmacher stepped to within two feet of John and stood relaxed, arms down at his sides. "Mark you me," he said again. He was watching John's eyes.

John was nearly two feet taller than Herdtmacher and was more than twice his weight. And he was undoubtedly a good amount stronger. But he knew, down deep where it burned and hurt like fire, that those things didn't matter. They didn't make any difference at all. Not against this man.

It was a long and heavy dagger he held, inlaid with tiny gems on the haft and comfortable in his hand. He looked down at it, then at Herdtmacher. He'd fought dozens of grown men over the years. He'd never been intimidated by any of them. They might be good men, they might be bad men. It never made any difference. When they stood against him they were just bodies, things he would overcome sooner or later. But this time wasn't anything like any of those times. This time everything was new. He felt as helpless as a baby. He felt like crying.

John closed his hand around the dagger. It seemed to belong there, like a natural extension of himself. And as fast as despair had hit him, anger did the same thing. Yes, he thought. The situation was different, and new: It wasn't just a beating and embarrassment he was risking. It was his family. This man was threatening his family.

His arm jumped of its own accord, lightning quick. The dagger was aimed at the man's midsection. Mentally John could feel the blow landing. He was hitting hard. But the inked dagger found only air, although Herdtmacher seemed not to have moved at all. At least, John's mind did not register any movement. The covered blade slid past Herdtmacher's stomach with an inch to spare. John reacted instantly. He planted his right foot, feinted with the dagger, and whipped out with his other arm, a hard backhand aimed at the man's head. Again, all he found was air.

John straightened up and jumped away, to his left. Herdtmacher moved with him and was in his original position again, two feet away in an arms-down, relaxed posture. The boy sank to a crouched stance and feinted again with the dagger. In the same movement he kicked the dirt and raised a small cloud of dust that reached his knees. He needed to score, even if he didn't hurt the Duelist. It was important to return some of Herdtmacher's intimidation. That would help to even things at the real fight. He used the momentary cover to scoop up some loose dirt with his left hand. He circled Herdtmacher slowly, with his clenched left hand just below the dagger-wielding right. Herdtmacher turned with him. John dropped his left hand and swung the dagger at the Duelist's face. When Herdtmacher ducked under the blow John brought up his left hand with the dirt in it.

Two iron vices closed around John's thick wrists, with Herdtmacher's palms over the backs of his hands. The Duelist bent his knees and pulled his elbows inward, rotating his hands around. To John's amazement his wrists gave way. A second later he was up on his toes, trying to get away from the excruciating pain. Herdtmacher rolled his shoulders, gently, and John cried out. The dirt and the dagger dropped to the ground.

When the pressure slackened, John jerked his hands away and made a grab for Herdtmacher's forearms. He caught them and held on with all the strength in his hands. He'd crushed dried firewood with the same grip. The flesh he was now gripping felt more like iron, than wood.

The Duelist smiled for the first time. "Goodt, Chon. Now?"

John yanked Herdtmacher toward him and kicked out at his stomach. His next sensation was of his hands closing on themselves, and of his foot twisting hard to the left. He jumped to stay with the foot. As he left the ground the Duelist caught him with a leg-sweep. John tumbled in the air and landed facedown in the dirt. He was up again instantly.

Herdtmacher stood exactly as before. The smile was still there, but he was shaking his head slowly. "Not daggers, I think. Too dancherous for you. This iss not to death." He thought for a few seconds. "Do you haff training with ax? Big man with ax iss goodt with small man and dagger. Exciting for watchers."

John was dusting himself off and catching his breath. "No," he said.

"Pike?" Herdtmacher picked up the dagger and wiped it clean before wrapping it again. "Sword?"

John shook his head. "I have no training, Mr. Herdtmacher. I'll use my hands."

Herdtmacher nodded. "Goodt hands, Chon. Strong. Fast. But no training. Herr Manley hass lied to me. He sass you are trained fighter."

"I'm experienced," John said. "I'll beat you. I have to."

"I haff signed already contract," Herdtmacher said. "Too late to say no. *Verstehen?* Wot will be, will be."

"Yes, sir. We all do what we have to do."

"Yes. Until again I will see you."

It occurred to John then, that he hadn't seen a flyer or a horse for Herdtmacher. He understood why when the Duelist turned and set off for Dennis Town at a strong, steady run.

John stared after him. Their meeting had changed everything. John saw the problem with a new clarity. A new focus. Manley wasn't going to attack him before the fight. There was no need to. A rabbit had a better chance against a mad lion, than an untrained boy had against a Grade One Expert Duelist. There had to be a way, though.

He kept watching until the Duelist was no longer visible. Noddy had been right. Herdtmacher was light-years beyond him. Beyond anything he had ever imagined. He'd give anything, except his family, to learn from Thomas Klaus Herdtmacher.

Dr. Samuels' idea had to work. Otherwise . . . otherwise, he told himself, I'll do what I have to do. And that's too bad. We could have been good friends.

He began running, taking his time. He didn't want to catch the Duelist. Not yet.

"You what?"

"Read it, Willie." John pulled the folded document from his shirt pocket and dropped it on the desk. Manley unfolded it and pulled his chair closer in. "I'll save you the trouble," John said, aping Manley's behavior of two nights before. "It says what I just told you. I've mortgaged the house, and the land."

"You can't," Manley snapped. "That property is registered to Gus. And, it's pledged as security for our bet."

John recited carefully. "Dr. Samuels will attest that Gus is incapacitated. As guardian of his estate I have every legal right to use his assets to pay for his medical expenses."

"Expenses?" Manley was turning red. "Your grandfather had an accident, boy. A few broken bones. How much can that cost? You could've come to me for help, and . . ." His eyes narrowed. "This is nonsense. I know the law. This is invalid." He threw the document toward John. "That property is pledged."

"Gus has no existing debt to you," John said. "And there's no certainty that he ever will. The property is therefore without encumbrance." He smiled down. "That's your copy," he said, pointing to the floor. "I suggest you read it."

The thug named Noddy had mentioned that his boss was prone to throwing fits. He was right. Manley was right, too, about the document. It was invalid. That's why it had cost so much, at Manley's expense, to have it drawn up by the woman and the sickly old man in Portside. Dr. Samuels had pointed out that Wilfred Manley was compulsive about details. He'd have the paper checked out immediately. So it would cost him even more money, to learn that it was a fraud. In the meantime Manley's joy in anticipating a big win was cut down a little. That was the whole point. Dr. Samuels had told him about two principles in war. Divide and conquer. Demoralize, then strike.

When Manley quieted down a little, John turned to the woman sitting behind him, on a plush green couch. "It's a shame Gus had that accident, Iris. This wouldn't have been necessary if he hadn't got hurt."

"That's right!" Manley screamed. "You—"

Iris ignored John and spoke calmly to Manley. "The house and the land are virtually worthless, Wilfred."

"I know that," Manley said heatedly. "It's the principle that bothers me. Having this . . . boy, think he can pull something on Wilfred Manley."

"It's the bets," Iris continued, "and the little girls who make this worthwhile. Isn't that right? And there's not a thing this dim-witted freak can do about that."

John flushed. He turned around and said to Manley, "She got the best of this partnership, didn't she? Your men think that's pretty funny, Willie. You should hear them laughing about it. Half the people in Portside are laughing about it too."

"That's another lie," Manley said in a husked-out whisper. "My men wouldn't laugh at me."

"Sure they wouldn't. Believe that if you want. Who cares, anyway? I don't. And neither does Iris. I've got my money now, Willie, like that paper says. And if I lose the fight you'll have to pay it back yourself. Out of your share of the winnings."

He turned and faced Iris again. "Maybe you'll pay, too. Maybe I'll win."

"So," she said. She was laughing at him. "You really think you can beat Cyclone Tom?"

John smiled at her. "What I think is that you're not half as smart as you believe you are. It was your plan, though, wasn't it? Willie met you somewhere and started whining like he always does. He told you how he wanted to get even with Gus. You worked out how he could do it, isn't that right?"

"Go on," Iris said. "You're really quite amusing."

"And I'll tell you what else I think, Iris. I think this midget is going to kill you, when your plan costs him

everything he owns." He bent double, bringing his face
to within an inch of hers. "Unless someone saves him
the trouble."

She was still smiling. John lowered his voice to a
whisper. "Too bad about Ko Kim messing up your tat-
too, Iris." She jerked a hand to her blouse sleeve and
went white as paint. Now she stared up at him, tight-
lipped and wide-eyed. It was all the confirmation John
needed. "But that's nothing compared to what's going
to happen to you. You're going to hurt, Iris." She
turned away. John continued whispering to her.
"You're going to hurt ten times more than Ko Kim ever
did. Are you listening, Iris?" He willed her to look up
at him again. To see her death in his eyes. When she refused to raise her eyes to his, he added, "It's all coming
to you. Not here. Not now. But soon."

John stood again and looked down at Manley. "You
made some mistakes, Willie. You're going to learn
about them one at a time. As a good friend of mine
would say," he switched to a low, guttural voice, "wot
you haff done iss dancherous for you. *Verstehen?*"

Manley jumped to his feet. "Who told you? One of
my men? Which one was it?"

John left them and slammed the door behind himself. At the bottom of the stairs he stopped to listen. The
man and the woman were exchanging threats and accusations at the top of their lungs. After a few minutes he
took the back way out into the scorching noonday heat.

Dr. William Samuels met John at the door of a small,
one-floor building that served as his home and office. It was also Dennis Town's only hospital. Samuels

was thirty. He was a small, studious-looking man and the only person John knew who could outrun him in a sprint. His problem, according to John, was that he had no endurance. After a mile Dr. Samuels was ready to faint. The physician was smiling when he greeted John and invited him inside. Dr. Samuels had only ninety-two days left on his eight-year contract to service Dennis Town. Every passing day seemed to widen his smile.

The first thing a visitor saw on entering Dr. Samuels' living area was a full-wall tapestry in the foyer. It was a landscape from his native world of Eusebeus. What always struck John about it was the cool gray sky and the abundance of trees. He couldn't imagine what it would feel like, smell like, to be surrounded by so much greenery. The landscape was alien, but very inviting. The tragedy was that this beauty would soon be gone forever. Terraformation on Eusebeus was failing. The forests were dying, and no one knew why. It was predicted that within twenty years the world would be nothing but desert again.

Dr. Samuels, like all of the remaining original colonists and the first and second-generation natives, planned to move on. But he wanted to be among the last to leave. And every moment on Janus prevented him from building a memory of his true home.

"How are you, John?" he asked, pumping the giant's hand vigorously. "Come in, come in!"

"Your beard's getting thicker," John said.

"So is your head, you charming liar." It was a running joke between them. Samuels had never been able to grow a full beard. What he managed to grow looked like scrub brush in the desert. John, on the other hand, was fourteen years old and needed to shave twice a day to be what Ko Kim called "presentable in society."

John noticed the small cap on the back of his friend's balding head. "Did I come at a bad time?"

"My congregation was here. They've both left now." He removed the yarmulke. "Gus and the twins are out back."

"You threw them out?" John asked with a smile.

"Actually, your aunts have been a great help. And your grandfather has been a model patient."

John looked at Samuels for long seconds. "I don't believe that," he said.

Dr. Samuels raised thick eyebrows, then burst out laughing. "Good. You're getting over your childish gullibility."

"Yes, sir," John said seriously, "I am, and very quickly."

"Did you show Manley the paper?"

"I just came from there."

"I have iced tea in the kitchen. Come sit, and tell me how it went."

Half an hour later Dr. Samuels looked up from his hands. He'd cried and laughed, both pretty hard, and he felt emotionally spent. "I'm truly sorry about Ko Kim, my friend. But you don't want to talk about her anymore, do you?"

"Not now, Doctor. I just wanted you to know what was happening."

"I understand."

"So, what do you think?"

"The phony mortgage has had some effect, judging by the way they argued as you were leaving. It's too early to tell how much, though. But that other thing, about Herdtmacher. I never thought Manley was that smart."

"I still don't think he is."

"You're probably right, it was Iris's idea. And it stinks. But from a dispassionate point of view, it's brilliant. Imagine! Everyone, you, me, and the town, thought you'd be fighting that Cyclone Tom. The bets have been made on that belief. And I can tell you, John, this is already the biggest gaming event in all the long years I've been here. But no one can claim fraud and pull out of the bet. As you point out, Manley never said that Herdtmacher and Cyclone Tom were the same man."

"I hope you didn't bet on me," John said.

"John, you look like a haunted man. I wish I could take that for you and carry it. But you know I don't make wagers. If I did, though, I'd bet on you. I don't care how good this Duelist is."

"You haven't seen him, Dr. Samuels. But I know you're speaking out of friendship, and I appreciate that." He took a long swallow of the iced tea and waved away a fifth refill.

"So what are you going to do?" Dr. Samuels asked.

"I have an idea. Will you tell me what you think of it?"

They talked for another half hour before walking out into the small fenced-in yard, what Dr. Samuels referred to as "the courtyard at Dennis Town's monument to the healing arts." Gus was snoring on a cot beneath the one tree. His arms and legs were cast in transparent plasticite and his chest was tightly bound with strips of white cloth. His hair was neatly cut and brushed, and he was clean-shaven for the first time John could remember. He looked ten years younger than he had.

The twins were sleeping on the brown grass on either side of Gus's cot. They had cut the legs and the midriff from their overalls, against the heat. They looked as if they'd been scrubbed with a strong soap.

John motioned his friend to silence and stood quietly, watching Gus and the twins for several minutes. In the kitchen again, he said, "I've never seen them like that before. Clean, happy-looking . . ." He put his hand on Dr. Samuels' shoulder, nearly covering it. "I'm going to pay you for this, sir. I'm going to—"

Dr. Samuels put his hand on top of John's. "I'll leave you alone for a few minutes. Go back out there and sit with your family, John. Then you have work to do. The fight's scheduled for tomorrow night."

He'd never cared much for alcohol, but this time John wasn't refusing any offers. Amy Lennox added another glass of beer to the seven already in front of him. "This one is from those two over there," she said. She pointed to a table near the bar's entrance. Two men smiled and raised their glasses to him. John nodded his thanks and turned around again.

Those two, and about a quarter of the people in The Pit, he'd never seen before. Word had spread: Wilfred Manley's been tricked into a sure-lose bet, and his money is there for the winning. No one seemed to mind that the price of drinks had gone up past double. There had been a line outside, waiting to get in. When they saw John coming, they broke out in applause and cheering. They made way for him and clapped him on the back and upper arms.

The room was cooler and more packed than he'd ever seen it, and the drinks began arriving the moment a man stood up and offered John his place at the bar. When Mary came downstairs to say hello, a woman embraced her and gave her some money. It was enough money to make her John's companion for the next twelve hours.

"This one's next, Big John," Mary said. She lifted a glass from the seven and set it next to his hand. She was sitting on the bar to his right, with her feet resting on his leg. "Thanks for letting me stay. I thought I'd be working all day again, it's been so busy down here and upstairs."

Through the wall to John's left came bursts of laughter and curses. Someone had either won or lost a fortune in the casino. He shouted to be heard above the wave of noise. "What? What did you say, Mary?"

"I said thanks for letting me—"

He nodded to her. "You're welcome. But I didn't pay, someone else did."

"What?"

"Never mind."

Mary talked on, leaning over several times to kiss his cheek. Every time she did that there was applause. That bothered John, the way everyone was watching everything she did for him. Her being naked like this in a room full of people wasn't her idea; they didn't have to treat her like some kind of cute pet. Seven of Manley's women were circulating around, serving drinks and talking and sitting with customers. They were naked, too, but no one was making a spectacle of them.

He tried to understand what she was saying. After a few minutes he gave up and began simply nodding or shaking his head, whichever seemed the right way to answer.

After an hour and twelve glasses of beer he judged the time to be right. John stood up, remembering to waver a little on his feet. He raised his hands over his head and lowered them, palms down. A few people understood what he was doing and were quiet for a few seconds. Then they were swept up again in celebrating or arguing, whatever they had been doing before he stood up.

After two more tries John climbed up on the bar. Heads turned in his direction. Glasses were raised and nearly everyone who was seated stood up and cheered. John tried to call out, but couldn't even hear himself. Miss Lennox tugged on his trousers leg. With gestures and carefully mouthed words she asked, "Do you want their attention?"

John nodded.

A second later the music speakers blared out a shrill tone that cut the air like a knife. Two hundred mouths snapped shut and half that number of patrons started for the exits.

"Wait!" Amy Lennox called. "Now just wait!" When the murmuring died down she said in a quieter voice, "It's not the Peacekeepers. Big John has something to say."

There was a quick round of cheering as John held up his hands. His fingers brushed against the sand-textured ceiling and for a moment he poked at it and grinned crookedly. When he looked down at the crowd,

he reeled, almost falling. These were things he'd seen
Gus do.

"My friends," he began. "That's right, you're my
friends."

"You know it, Big John!"

"Remember me? We're like brothers!"

"But there's some here I never met before," the giant
continued. "So let me introduce myself." He paused
dramatically and then flexed his arms and threw a
quick roundhouse punch at the air. "I am Big John!"

The crowd clapped and hooted, calling out his name.
This was all part of the plan he'd discussed with Dr.
Samuels. The one thing he hadn't thought of was that
he'd enjoy performing this much, and that he'd get so
much back. He put that aside and went on. "Someone
told me that a few of you are betting a little money on
me. Is that right?"

"Yes!"

"More than a little, my whole store!"

"Do it for us, Big John!"

"Well, I'm happy that you put so much faith in me.
Especially those of you who've been so kind to my
family over the years." A few of the patrons looked
down at the floor. Most accepted the remark at face
value and applauded themselves. That made it easier
for John to keep going. "You all know that I'm going to
win, is that right?"

The room shook, with all the stomping and yelling.

John waited for the noise to ease down and counted
slowly to five. "Unfortunately," he said, "so do Wilfred
Manley and his partner, Iris." He stopped and watched
their faces. Then he lowered his eyes and breathed out
a loud sigh.

A woman called out in the thick silence. "What in hell are you talking about, John?"

"I'm sorry," John said. "I am awfully sorry, my friends. But I suppose you ought to hear it from me first. Wilfred Manley and his partner Iris realized I was going to win. So they have canceled the fight. That means all bets are voided. There will be no winnings for you. No money. Wilfred Manley beat you again."

This time the silence was like cement. John saw six men, among them Keeler and his brother Wolf, get up from their table and run outside.

"That's right, my friends," John called out. "Wilfred Manley and his partner Iris have ended it before they lost any money. So just pay for your drinks and go home. That's on the orders of Wilfred Manley and Iris. Get out now, or they will personally come down those stairs," he said, pointing out the window and across Carney Street, "and throw all of you in the street."

The quiet that was like cement cracked down the middle. People in the crowd looked at one another and turned, as a unit, toward the door. Some of them picked up chairs and began dismembering the barroom. John jumped down from the bar and tucked Mary under one arm. Amy Lennox ducked into the safe box beneath the bar and locked it. By now chairs and tables were flying and the sound was like continuous thunder. People were four abreast, leaving the bar for Manley's offices across the street. John ran for the nearest window, kicked it apart, and climbed through. Outside, he set Mary on her feet. They sprinted away to the sounds of breaking glass and shattering furniture. John heard a man scream, and then he and Mary rounded the corner and slowed to a walk.

The flyer was waiting where Gus had usually left it. John got it started and made one pass over The Pit. Half the crowd was in the street now, broken up into smaller groups. They seemed to be lost, milling around in circles. As if waiting for someone to point out what else Manley owned so they could break it. The other buildings on the block would be safe, John knew. He guessed it would be about an hour before the first Peacekeepers arrived from New Cardiff. An hour or so later there would be sixty to eighty of them in three or four armed scouters from Portside. His hope was that by the time they got there it would all be over.

Dr. Samuels was waiting with the twins outside his living quarters. John went inside with him. They came out a minute later carrying Gus on a stretcher. After he was loaded through the rear door, the twins and Dr. Samuels climbed in. As soon as the four new passengers were strapped in John took off. He climbed almost vertically to cruising altitude, and leveled off.

"So," came Dr. Samuels' voice as the physician moved from the rear of the flyer, "I can hear the party from here. What—" He stopped talking and blushed crimson when he saw Mary strapped in beside John.

"Ho, Bill," she said.

"Uh, ho," Samuels said. He removed his white smock and passed it to her.

Mary covered herself and frowned. "You don't like me anymore?"

The twins slid into the rear seat, giggling. John turned and glared them into silence. He looked thoughtfully at his friend the physician for a few seconds, then glanced downward. It was time to begin the descent.

After dinner Glenda and Brenda went back to Gus's room to see if the old man was awake yet. Dr. Samuels told John he'd left his radio in the flyer and was going outside to use it. "I want to contact the Peacekeepers. The trouble should be over by now and they might need me."

Half an hour later he reentered the kitchen. "There are a few injuries," he said. "Thankfully, nothing too serious. Apparently the Peacekeepers got there less than an hour after the trouble started. I can wait if you don't want to take me back to the hospital yet."

"What about Manley and Iris?"

"Our friend Wilfred suffered three broken teeth and a fractured jaw. They're keeping him sedated until I get there." He smiled at John and sat down across the table from him. "As I said, there's no reason to hurry."

"And Iris?"

"She apparently escaped any harm. There were only two women hurt, minor scratches, and I know both of them." He blushed again and reached for an empty cup in front of him. "I mean, they're both miners I've treated before."

"Too bad Iris wasn't hurt," Brenda said. She and Glenda took seats at the table again.

Glenda agreed. "I'm going to ride Hershel right over her for what she did to Poppa."

And Sister Kim, John added silently. "What else did the Peacekeepers say, Doctor?"

"This is boring," Glenda said. "We're going to visit Ling-Ling."

"Be careful," John told them. "It's dark."

"We don't need you to be our mother," Brenda said. "So stop it, is that all right?"

"You just fight," Glenda said. "That's what you know how to do."

When they'd gone, Dr. Samuels said, "The Peace-keepers asked me if I knew how that rumor started. The one about Manley 'and his partner Iris' canceling the fight. That was a good idea, by the way. It's only bad luck that it didn't have the effect we wanted."

"What did you tell the Peacekeepers?"

"I told them I'd heard it around town somewhere, and may have mentioned it to you. But I couldn't remember for sure."

"What did they say?"

"Not much, John."

John let go a sigh. "The idea," he said, "was that they would cancel the fight because of all the trouble. They didn't say anything about that?"

"I gave them my recommendation, as I'd told you I would. I went further, and told them I'd file a complaint with the town's Common Law Council for reckless endangerment if they don't stop this before it gets worse."

"That should have worked, Doctor. You're a member of the Council."

"So is Wilfred Manley, John. And besides that, I'm only one of seven. And it seems . . ."

"Go ahead. Please."

"It seems that a great number of the Peacekeepers have made bets. Some for you, some against. And so have other units, in other districts. Their headquarters are even taking bets over the radio." He pushed the cup to the center of the table and looked up into John's eyes. "This is bigger than anyone could have predicted, John. Apparently the news is all over Janus. The Peace-keepers told me there are five passenger ships coming to Dennis Town before dawn tomorrow."

"Media?"

"Precisely. That's why the Peacekeepers got here so quickly, by the way. They were packed and ready to go when the call came in."

"So all of this means . . ."

"I don't want to say it either, John. I cannot express how sorry I am. And I'll keep trying, I promise you that. But as of this moment the fight is on for tomorrow night. As scheduled."

John looked at his friend for a few seconds, then nodded. A cold serenity settled over him, like ice on the mountains. "I see." That was it, then. It was settled. The young giant sighed. "What must be, must be," he said.

Four fist-sized stones lay three feet apart on flat ground. With less than a second's lapse in time the first, second, and fourth burst apart in an explosion of dust.

"Damn it, boy, you missed one again!" Gus leaned back from the tripod-mounted binoculars and spit in the dirt. John noted that Gus was moving pretty well, despite the four casts and the bandage around his chest. That didn't come as a surprise. On the ride back to town Dr. Samuels had told him three or four times to make sure Gus stayed in bed for a few more days. He didn't know the old man very well.

"Poppa," Glenda said, "the spread's set too narrow. He could get them all with one shot if he'd do what you told him."

"I know that, stupid," Gus snapped at her. "He won't listen. He never did listen to me."

"That's right," Brenda said to her twin. "Poppa's told him, over and over. It's not Poppa's fault if John won't listen."

"I never said—"

"Set them up again," John said.

Glenda galloped away on Rubin with a bag of stones. When she came back and climbed down, John slapped the stock of the Barrow rifle to his shoulder and fired four times.

"All four!" Gus called out.

"Again," John said.

He hit all four the next three times, then two, then four twice again.

Gus leaned back and moaned while he settled into his padded chair. "Good enough," he said. "You'll get him."

"Not good enough," John said. "I have to place the shot exactly."

"I know that, boy."

"No you don't, Gus. You want me to widen the beam. And if I do that I'll probably kill him. It's got to be like a needle, or I won't do it. And it's got to be exact."

"And suppose he's moving?" Gus asked. "How are you going to be exact then?"

It was always this way, arguing with Gus. The old man knew the right way to do everything, and anything else was stupid. It was even worse, now that he was sober. At least when he was drunk he'd pass out after a while.

"I don't want to murder him," John said again.

"I know that, John," Gus said in a reasonable tone. "I raised you, so I know how you are. But if he beats you we lose everything. And the girls go to that place. Is that what you want, John?"

John gritted his teeth. "What in the name of hell does it matter what I want? When has that ever mattered?"

"Ho, just a minute," Gus said indignantly. "I spent time and money raising—"

"You made that stupid bet, Gus. You! You bet the house and the land, and your daughters. Your own daughters! You're selling them to be whores! And now you want me to murder an innocent man, and probably be executed, because of your stupidity!"

Glenda punched his leg with balled fists. "Don't you talk to Poppa like that! All he did is try to make us rich."

"And look what they did to him," Brenda said. "All you have to do is fight. Why are you being such a coward?"

Mary spoke up for the first time. She was wearing a set of work clothes Gus hadn't worn in years. The way they hung on her made her look even smaller next to John than she usually did. "I don't think that's fair," she said. "Mr. Herdtmacher is a real Duelist."

"He won't be for long," Gus said. "At least, not a dangerous one. Isn't that right, John?"

John stood up and looked down at his grandfather. Gus was his own flesh. The same blood ran through both of them. He didn't understand how the old man could . . . but the idea to shoot Herdtmacher is yours, he told himself, not his. Give yourself time and you'll be him.

John shrunk back from his thoughts in disgust. The
anger drained out of him like water from the Farnham
River in winter. My idea, not his. He felt limp and exhausted. "I'm not afraid," he said quietly. "Not the way
you think. I'm not fighting for myself. And no one, not
Herdtmacher or Manley, is really fighting against me.
They're doing what they think they have to do, to get
what they think they need. Like everyone else." He
hadn't told them about Iris and Ko Kim. He knew he
wouldn't be able to take their indifference.

"It's my job to beat them. That's all this is, just another job for me to do." He looked at each of the three
faces he'd seen every day, for so many years. It felt like
looking at strangers. "So I'll do it, just as well as I can.
But when this is over I'm leaving Dennis Town. I'm
going to Portside to look after Ko Kim, and I won't be
back."

Gus looked up at him with a startled expression.
"I'm hurt, boy. Can't you see that? I'm a man, and I can
take whatever comes. Everybody knows that about me.
Whatever comes, I take it and I don't complain. But my
girls need you. You can't leave them."

"Poppa, don't beg," Brenda said. "We don't need
him. Not after we're rich."

"That's right," Glenda said. "Maybe he should go.
Everybody knows he doesn't belong here. That's why
he gets in trouble all the time. And we can take care of
you, anyway. Better than anyone else ever could."

Gus smiled up at John. This time his expression was
triumph. "You're of age, John. You can do what you
want to. Whatever you think is right. For everybody."

John turned away from them. He was whipped more

surely than any Duelist could do it. He began a slow walk toward the house.

"Come back here and take your whore with you!" Glenda said angrily. "And she can burn those clothes of Poppa's. He'll never wear them again!"

Mary spun around on her. "Little princess," she said, "I wasn't much older than you two are, when Manley started me. Before that I used to come visit. Do you remember that?"

"No, I don't."

"You wouldn't. I was somebody else then, and that person is dead in everyone's mind. That's what happens when you go there. You're not the little friend who comes over and plays with a man's children anymore. Now you're something he can use to make himself feel good. Not anything human anymore. John still remembers who I was when I visited you. He stops by and talks to me like he did then. But no one else ever does. No one else ever did. Not just to talk."

"So?" Brenda asked. "You're a whore, like Ko Kim. What do you expect people to do?"

Mary's eyes filled with tears. "Nobody deserves what happened to me. But if anybody did, it would be you two. And Gus."

Glenda said, "You get out of here!"

Mary had more to say. But she turned away and caught up with John. "Will you take me back now?"

"That's a bad idea. Manley will think you're on my side."

"He won't do anything to me. I'm prime stock."

"Mary, I took you out of there because I didn't want you to get hurt. That makes you my responsibility for now. You can stay here."

"No, I can't. And neither can you."

"I have to. This is my home."

"And you're being used the same way I am. In my home."

John stopped and looked down at her. "What do you mean? I'm not a . . ." Then he laughed. "I guess I am, at that! That's exactly what I am. But I'm not as pretty as you, Mary. It's a wonder I make a living at all."

"Thank you for the compliment. But don't underrate yourself."

They walked into the house, still laughing at each other. "So," John said, "I guess you finally did teach me something about growing up."

Mary stopped laughing and stepped up close to him. "I care about you, John. You've known that for a long time. And there is a lot more I can teach you."

He took her hands, but was too embarrassed to be serious about it. "Thanks. But I have to be somewhere else tonight."

She pulled her hands away. "John, no one ever asks me what I think. Except you, I mean. And you didn't ask this time, but I'm going to tell you anyway. Everything is wrong about this. Not just the fight, but what you're planning to do."

"I know that."

"If you fight Herdtmacher and lose, you'll still be alive. He's a professional and he knows you can't hurt him. He'll stop when it's clear to the judge that you can't fight anymore."

"I know that too. And thanks for the confidence in me."

"I won't let you change the subject, so don't pretend

to be a baby. What I mean is, that Duelist won't kill you. But if you shoot him before the fight—"

"I'm not going to kill him. I told Gus that. You heard me."

"You can't guarantee it, though, can you?"

"No."

"And even if you don't, you'll cripple him. He's not a bad man, John. He's never done anything to hurt you. I don't think you could live with that."

"Mary, he's a threat to my family. It's not his fault, but he is. I have to defend my family."

Mary shook her head and looked angrier than he'd ever seen her. "No you don't. They're not worth it. I never thought I'd say that about any family, because a family is what I've wanted more than anything since Manley made me a whore. But I'm saying it now. They're not worth it, John. I'm sorry, but they're not."

"I think you're wrong. But even if you're not it doesn't matter. They're mine, and my responsibility."

"All right. Let that go. Think about this, then. Think about what this will do to you. Inside, I mean. You'll never be the same person again. And I know something about that."

"I have to. I said before, this isn't about me. Not really."

"Yes, it is!" She set her jaw firm and put her hands on her hips. It was exactly what Ko Kim had done when she needed to yell at Gus. "Listen to me, even if you never do again. I want you to picture Herdtmacher. Just the way he is, the way you described him to me. Now think about Cyclone Tom and the way he is." She stopped talking and waited for him to answer.

"I don't think I understand," he said after a while.

"You do too," she said in a quieter voice. "If you don't, you will. I just hope it's not too . . ." She turned away and crossed the room. "I'm going home. I can walk, but I'd appreciate a ride. I'll wash Gus's clothes and get them back to him."

"You don't need to do that. They're old."

Mary looked back over her shoulder. There were tears in her eyes again. "I don't want a ride, after all."

Seven times he set the flyer down a hundred yards ahead of her, and six times she walked past him. On the seventh she ran the last fifty yards, laughing. She jumped in beside him and kissed his cheek. "I'm sorry," she said. "It's selfish to give you so much to worry about right now."

"I know why you did, and I appreciate it."

She talked most of the way to Dennis Town, going on happily about things they both liked. Then she glanced behind the seat and saw the Barrow rifle with its hunting scope attached. After that she was quiet.

"No, Big John," the miner said. She wiped her mouth with black-stained fingers. "I've seen a man exactly like that, but I don't know where he's staying. Is he one of the media people?"

John shrugged. They'd all learn who Herdtmacher was tonight, at the fight. He decided to let them all be shocked at once. Maybe they'd go after Manley and Iris again. And do the job right this time.

The miner grinned and took another swallow of beer. "I just hope he and his cohorts stay awhile afterwards. I want a holo of me and my new flyer to be seen all over Janus." She bit into a boiled potato and chewed contentedly. "This is going to be the best night of me and Henry's life. I know I'm lucky to have a job, with just about all the mines closed until the market opens up again. But Manley never did pay much, and it's half that now. Now things are going to be different. And it's all thanks to you. Can I order you some food? I'd offer beer, but we need you all there tonight."

"No, but thanks."

"I can get you that girl from yesterday again. She's little enough to offer, I guess."

"I don't want anything."

"I understand. I'd be a little nervous too. Did you see how the streets are about empty?"

John had, and it was eerie. He hadn't seen anyone, flying into town. After he'd let Mary off and walked her upstairs to her room he stood outside the door to see if there was going to be any trouble. The only people he saw were Wolf and Keeler. They walked past him in the hallway with a polite nod. Wolf said, "It was you, not her." And that was all. Outside he'd been accosted by a team of media people with cameras and questions. He scowled and walked at them with his fists clenched. They made way, and didn't follow him around to The Pit. Except for the media people and Miss Lennox and this one miner, the town looked empty.

"Everybody's resting up for the celebration." The miner swallowed, and spit on the floor. "I wish I knew what got that rumor started yesterday. You looked awfully upset when you told everyone about it."

"I guess you hear things that aren't true," John said. He stood up and pushed the stool back under the table. This was a waste of precious time. The contest with

Grade One Expert Duelist Thomas Klaus Herdtmacher was only six hours away.

"You're right about that." The miner raised her mug and finished the beer. "I only believe what I see, and only half of that. You sure you don't want some food or a girl or something? Maybe it'll settle you for the fight."

"Thanks anyway."

John found the Duelist from the air, only a few minutes later. As soon as he was sure of who it was he tossed the binoculars on the empty seat beside him and circled away in a wide arc. Herdtmacher was standing in an abandoned soya field six miles south of town. There was a line of trees half a mile further south. John flew five miles beyond that, then circled back to the north at just above ground level. He set the flyer down behind the trees and got out with the field glasses slung over one shoulder and the Barrow rifle tucked under the other. Hunting was one thing Gus had taught him well.

The low-grown vegetation made foot travel difficult but provided good cover. For the last eighth of a mile he crouched down and moved at a steady, silent stalking pace. He circled to the west and made the approach from downwind of his quarry, keeping the early afternoon sun behind him. He was able to close within three hundred yards of Herdtmacher before his hunter's sense told him not to go any further. Herdtmacher probably had an acutely developed ear. And just beyond where John was at that moment, the growth began to taper off gradually for thirty more yards, where it became too short for concealment. This would have to do. John found a shallow depression behind a rotting log and lay in it, not moving for ten minutes. When everything felt right he raised himself slightly and put the binoculars to his eyes.

The Duelist was wearing a gray loincloth and working through a set of exercises. Moving slowly, John lowered the glasses and raised the rifle to his shoulder. He felt with his right thumb to check that the beam was set to minimum spread. At this distance the penetration diameter would be less than an eighth of an inch. He adjusted the scope for range and peered through it, taking a deep breath and holding it. His finger eased over the trigger guard.

Herdtmacher looked thinner than he had before, in the tunic. Or maybe it was that John expected to see bulging muscles, and didn't. The man looked . . . streamlined. That was the best word he could think of. The Duelist snapped from one position to another at a regular beat of one movement per second. Each position was rock-steady and perfectly balanced. Like a statue, John thought.

He watched, fascinated. None of the Duelist holos he'd seen had shown anything like this. He felt as if he were watching a secret ritual that only the initiates, the Duelists, were permitted to know or to see. His finger raised from the trigger guard. After a few minutes, Herdtmacher's pattern of movement changed. Now he was moving slowly, fluidly, as if he were underwater. His hands were open and he kept reaching for air, taking it and pulling it toward himself. Then he froze his upper body and gradually raised his left leg, knee straight, until his foot pointed at the sky and his shin rested against his forehead. He did the same thing on the right side and then nine more times for each leg.

A sudden breeze threw sand in John's face. He lowered the Barrow and wiped his eyes clear. When he positioned the rifle again Herdtmacher was sitting cross-legged in the dirt, facing directly away from John. It was perfect. An easy shoulder shot, on each side. Just enough to even the fight. Or to call it off. There was no penalty for Manley if the fight were postponed or canceled. That penalty belonged only to Gus. And through him, John. Two shoulder shots was ideal. Chances were good that there would be no permanent damage. Two taps of his finger and it would be over. A year or two in prison if he was caught, but he wouldn't be caught. He took in another deep breath and held it. His finger found the trigger, and he slowly released the breath.

Herdtmacher began leaning slowly to his right. John followed the movement in the scope's cross hairs. No problem. He tightened his finger and Herdtmacher reversed direction. It became a pattern, with the Duelist rocking from side to side, faster every time. This went on for several minutes. Finally Herdtmacher stopped moving. He took five long, deep breaths. Then his head lowered forward and he appeared to fall asleep.

The young giant inhaled again and prepared to shoot. He sighted carefully and drew in one final deep breath. It would be painful, he knew that. But he was sure that Herdtmacher had been hurt worse. Besides, everyone knew that pain meant nothing to Duelists. And besides that, too, Herdtmacher would probably do the same thing if he was in John's position.

Don't be absurd unless you mean to be. A Duelist would never do this.

But I'm not a Duelist. This isn't about money, or

rank. This is about my family. A man does what he has
to. What's right for his family. Sometimes people get in
the way. No one's fault. It's like Mary said. Everyone
gets used, for somebody else's benefit. That's not my
idea, it's just the way it is.

Is that what Mary was saying? Is that what Sister
Kim would say?

John shook his head, hard. He eased his finger back
in the guard and exhaled slowly, squeezing the trigger
as softly as he'd tickle a newborn chick. Just the way
Gus taught him.

Of its own accord his thumb twitched up and clicked
the Barrow onto safety. John jerked his head back, un-
sure of what had just happened. The safety was not supposed to be on. He released it, disgusted with his
weakness, and bent forward to the scope again.

Herdtmacher was standing, looking straight at him.

It's still easy. He's not moving.

But this time John told his thumb what to do. He
lowered the rifle and got up on his feet. The two looked
at each other from a distance of three hundred yards.
Neither one of them moved until long minutes had
passed. Then Herdtmacher bent at the waist and bowed.

Somehow the Duelist had known he was there. If
he'd fired, would the focused beam have reached its
target? Nothing could move faster than light; Herdtmacher could not have dodged away. But somehow . . .
somehow, and John desperately wanted to know how,
he'd have moved out of the way a fraction of a second
before John squeezed the trigger. Of that, John was certain. Herdtmacher had known. That was knowledge
John would give his life to possess, if only for a day.
Just to know. Just to be, that good. But even if such a

bargain could be reached, he didn't have the price. His life wasn't his.

John turned away. He kicked the field glasses off into the distance and snapped the Barrow in half over his knee. He threw the pieces into the dirt and walked back to the flyer.

He thought he might circle Dennis Town for a while before setting down. A last few moments of peace, and then get on with whatever came up as the next best idea. Maybe there wasn't one. But a few moments of peace would be good.

One look down at The Pit, though, and John changed his mind. It looked like another riot had broken out. He left the flyer behind the boarded-up Mining Exchange and trotted three blocks toward the center of town. He didn't see anyone until he approached The Pit. Rounding the last corner, he was hit by a wall of noise. Carney Street was jammed with people. They were shouting and shaking their fists, looking up and pointing toward the office Manley kept above the barroom. John skirted around the crowd and made his way into the alley he and Mary had used as an escape route the day before. Today it was some kind of staging area, full of Peacekeepers.

"You're Big John, aren't you?" It was said by a helmeted Peacekeeper, the first in line of about twenty of them, all dressed in full riot gear. She was wearing a lieutenant's insignia.

"Connie, look at him," a man behind her said. "Who else could that be?"

"What's going on?" John called out to the woman.

"Another stupid question," the man said.

"You can go in," Connie said. "But you stay on the ground floor. Understand?"

"I understand, Lieutenant. But why all the trouble?"

"You've been out of town?"

"Yes, for a while." After leaving Herdtmacher in the soya field he'd flown aimlessly for about an hour, out over land that no one had settled on yet. He spotted a nice location for a cabin. It was close enough that he could check on Gus and the twins every week or so, and far enough away that the rest of the days would be his own. That was assuming his aunts didn't go to the bordello. Then he'd be in prison, waiting to be executed for killing Wilfred Manley. Or Iris, or both.

"The Council's meeting inside, upstairs. Last word I got is that the vote's tied at three to three."

John felt his pulse quickening. "Is this about the fight?"

"What else is going on in the world? Yes, it's about the fight. Word got out about an hour ago that the man you're fighting isn't the one everyone thought."

"Then they might call it off."

"Like I said, the vote's tied. That mob out front is the people who bet on you. That's just about the whole town, plus a few hundred more. Half want their money back and no fight. The other half says you'll win anyway, so let it happen. But if you lose they're going to be on the same side. There'll be a riot like no one's ever thought of before."

"Is there a time they have to decide by?"

"We should know soon," the lieutenant said. "A man named Samuels is on his way to cast the deciding vote. We're the last part of his escort."

"Samuels?" It had to be. Dr. Samuels had done it! "Dr. William Samuels?"

"That's the name I've got," she said.

John felt the world rising like air from his shoulders. He knew there was something he should say. It didn't matter if it was to two Peacekeepers he'd never seen before. Something should be said to mark this minute, this hour. In the happiest day of his life. He'd almost destroyed it all by shooting Herdtmacher. Why hadn't he listened to Mary? And he'd given up on the best friend he had. Why hadn't he trusted Dr. Samuels? Today would be a lesson. He needed to say something to mark it. But the words wouldn't come.

The lieutenant looked him up and down. "Now that I've seen you, I don't think there'll be any trouble. If you fight, you'll win."

"Thanks."

"But if you don't fight you'll lose the chance to be famous all over Janus. And beyond that, probably."

"I'll bear it," John said.

"That's the best way to look at it. How big are you, anyway?"

John laughed. "I never thought this way before, but maybe I'm just the right size, after all."

"What does that mean?"

The Peacekeeper behind her said, "That doesn't make any sense, boy."

"I know." Laughing was easier than it had been for a long time. It wasn't much to say to mark the moment, and the man was right. It didn't make any sense. But it would do. Maybe he'd build that cabin, after all.

Inside The Pit he sat drinking iced tea and enjoying the cool air. Dennis Town was going to be different

from this day on, he knew. Those people on Carney
Street were proof of that. With no fight, they'd get their
money back. Some would be disappointed, and some
would be relieved. But every person out there knew
that Manley had tried to cheat them out of what little
they had. They wouldn't let it go. Not this time. Wilfred
Manley would have to leave. Now there was only Iris
to deal with.

The door to the alley opened and the noise from outside rushed in. The Peacekeeper lieutenant came
through the door, followed by ten of her troops march-
ing two abreast. At the center of the formation was Dr.
Samuels. John stood and waved. "There's a pitcher of
tea here when you're through," he called out. The
young physician had his head down and his hands over
his ears, and didn't hear. The lieutenant and three more
Peacekeepers escorted him up the stairs.

"I'm sorry, but I'll need money for that tea," Amy
Lennox said from behind the bar.

"I will be very, very happy to pay," John said. Miss
Lennox had just acknowledged what he already knew.
It was over. He was just John again, and that felt fine.
He sat down and stretched his legs over the next three
stools. The cabin was already taking shape in his mind.
Maybe Mary would come out and visit sometimes.
Maybe she'd stay. She'd be surprised, how well he
could build. And that wasn't all. He knew more about
being grown up than she thought he did. A smile
formed on his face as he reached for the pitcher and
poured the glass full again.

Twenty minutes later the four Peacekeepers walked
back down the stairs. John jumped to his feet and
waited for his friend.

The lieutenant walked over to the bar and asked for a glass of beer.

"Where's Dr. Samuels?" John asked.

"He went out the front stairs," she said. "The crowd's watching the alley now. I'm giving him fifteen minutes to get away before I make the announcement."

"I didn't think of that. Thank you."

"It's my job." She accepted the beer and raised it to him. "So you're the first to hear the good news, Big John. The fight starts in one hour."

They'd taken down three old toolsheds and removed the entire back wall from the brothel. Perched at the edge of the ceiling/floor that divided the two levels was a row of plush chairs with small serving tables between them. Facing in the same direction on the ground below were another six rows of seats, and behind them ten more extended back into the lower level of the building.

A series of whistles sounded and thirty Peacekeepers backed away from their positions. The crowd streamed past them, racing for the best positions. Those who'd bought the seats filed into them. The rest were shoving one another and jostling with the Peacekeepers who now formed a line to keep them from blocking the view from the seats.

John pushed his way through the crowd, which seemed like a single, living, ugly thing. He ignored the cheers and the slaps on the back. This was a walking dream. It had to be. How could his friend, the only one besides Mary he had in Dennis Town . . . how could he do this? Gus, the twins, himself, they all stood to lose everything now. But maybe . . . wait a second, of course! The vote was tied, three to three. Manley must have bribed two of those three. Or threatened them. That had to be it.

At the center of the crowd two small boys were following a line in the dirt with paint dispensers. When they'd finished, they left behind them a thirty-foot white ring. The combat circle. Exactly the same size as every Duelist combat circle ever made on eight hundred other worlds. It was a link to the entire Great Domain. For now, Janus was part of something. Dennis Town was important. Once the ring was painted the crowd moved back of its own accord. No one would trespass this particular sanctity.

"Ho, Big John!"

The young giant turned his head and saw Wilfred Manley mount the center chair on the second floor. Even beneath the bandage he wore, his wide grin came through. Next to him Iris took her seat. She smiled and arched an eyebrow, nodding regally.

John ignored them and turned away. Gus and his aunts hadn't come. If they had, he'd have heard Gus bellowing by now. He was a little surprised to realize that he'd wanted them to be there. He scanned the opened-out room and the crowd, hoping to see Dr. Samuels or Mary. Neither was to be seen, but that didn't mean they weren't there. The crowd was just too big.

He'd never seen this many people together before. About half of the faces he saw were familiar. Scanning them, it seemed strange that the word "friend" never came to mind. Even so, it should have felt good, knowing that so many people had come to see him. Most of those who lived in or near Dennis Town were betting on him. That should feel good, too. But none of it did. The people were there to get some of Wilfred Manley's money. The fact that John's family was at stake . . . or that he could easily be crippled for life . . . That wouldn't slow down their enjoyment for a second. He wondered if Duelists felt that way before a death match. That could explain why they were famous for being unapproachable. Maybe it wasn't ego, after all. Maybe it was exactly what he felt. Whatever that was.

He shrugged it all off and removed his shirt and boots. A feeling of serenity, cold but comforting, settled over him. He welcomed it gratefully. What would be, would be. No more waiting.

When he stepped into the combat circle the crowd erupted. It sounded like the heaviest rain he'd ever heard, with people screaming over it. He was surprised again when it became a physical sensation. Pleasant, really, but still distant. The seconds passed and the roar grew even stronger until the feeling was about the same as when Ko Kim had taken him to Portside and stood with him in the ocean's waves. Each one lifted him and carried him somewhere. This was the same, with each wave of sound lifting him higher than the last, carrying him somewhere he'd never been or even imagined. He turned around in a slow circle and looked at their faces again. They still weren't his friends. He owed them nothing. But the sound of them felt good. It felt damned good.

Answer them, a familiar voice whispered in his mind. Answer them, Brother John.

He waved to them now, still turning in place to face them all. The waves broke higher, and better. Now he stepped to the center of the circle and flexed his arms. The response was deafening. He threw vicious punches at them in the air, and was drenched in the hysterical joy the crowd threw back at him.

The cacophony soared and crested, then collapsed in a fraction of a second. The silence hung in the air and seemed like a living thing itself. Then the noise built again, but it was different. The crowd was jeering. Screaming obscenities. John turned around to face the direction they were pointing.

Thomas Klaus Herdtmacher walked silently toward the ring, behind a phalanx of Peacekeepers. His face wore the same impassive look it had when John first saw him sitting at his kitchen table. He nodded a brief acknowledgment to the few who cheered for him. Herdtmacher was wearing a royal blue robe lined with a white cord. Around his neck on a platinum chain hung the Duelist Medallion. It was a circle of gold, seven inches in diameter and gleaming like a star. Embossed on it was the crossed pike-and-sword family crest of Admiral Simon Barrow, founder of the Duelists. Below the crest were the Roman numerals, CCCXV. Thomas Klaus Herdtmacher had killed three hundred fifteen times, in personal combat. Only death matches were recorded on the Duelist Medallion.

John took a deep breath and swallowed hard. It was difficult, suddenly, to keep his knees steady. His mind searched frantically for something to do, something to hide the terror that swept over him like one of the ocean waves he had ridden just moments before. The Duelist was moving so slowly it would take him forever to get to the combat circle. No, that was an illusion. Herdt-

macher was moving at a steady stride. And fast. Much
too fast.

Sister Kim whispered the answer. It will delight
your friends, Brother John. And make your enemies
crazy.

The young giant threw back his head, and he roared
with all his strength. Every eye there snapped toward
him, every face reflected shock. John roared again and
pawed at the air. He stamped the ground, raising a billow of dust, and roared for a third time.

The hunters in the crowd recognized the image. He
was creating a mountaintooth, the created beast, a ge-
netic experiment of the last century that had lived and
reproduced. The hunters cheered above all the rest. A
mountaintooth was the ultimate challenge. Some of
them joined in the pantomime, and the absurdity spread
until the sound could have been heard from miles away.
But no one was that far away. John looked up at Wilfred Manley. The little man's grin that showed through
the bandages before was gone.

As fast as it had started, the crowd noise died and
was gone.

Herdtmacher stepped inside the combat circle and
removed the medallion. He wrapped the chain protectively around the gold and touched it to his forehead
before sliding it into a maroon cloth case, and then into
a pocket of his robe. One of the Peacekeepers stood
outside the circle and waited while the Duelist removed
his robe and handed it to her. The loincloth he wore was
of the same royal blue as the robe. Herdtmacher took
two long strides toward John and stopped.

John roared again, stepping high as he walked out to
meet the Duelist. Only a few cheered this time. John

stopped three yards from Herdtmacher and glared down at him as hard as he could. The Duelist nodded. There was a quick flash of amusement in the impassive gray eyes before they went cold.

John almost jumped at the sound of a voice behind him.

"Gentlemen."

He turned around and saw a white-haired man holding a thick piece of paper. "I am Muhammad Kenyata, sirs," he said. "I am a native of Earth. I have been retained to act as sole referee for this bout. My qualifications include my having been a district judicial magistrate for sixty-three years in my home world. I have written three volumes on the art and the ethics of personal combat. I have officiated at one hundred seventeen Duelist matches. An affidavit is on file in your capital city of Portside, affirming that I have no financial or other interest whatsoever in the outcome of this match. Do you both accept me?"

"Yes, sir."

"I also."

"Thank you." Kenyata read from the document. "'This contest between Thomas Klaus Herdtmacher and John Biggle, Domain-Common date and year August 6, 2284, hour and location as listed above, is declared nonlethal and will be decided by a single judge. The combat will proceed without weapons other than those which are systemic to the human body.' Young man, do you know what that means?"

"Yes, sir. Hands and feet."

Kenyata looked up at John uncertainly. "It means hands, feet, elbows, knuckles, toes, knees, chin, head, teeth—"

"I understand, sir."

"Very well. After each two minutes the combatants will be afforded fifty seconds of rest outside the combat circle. The match will end, and the winner will be declared, when one is physically unable to continue." He looked at Herdtmacher, then at John. "That decision is to be made by me. There will be no appeal. Have you any questions?"

"Sir," John said, "I've never done this before."

"Yes, I am aware of that. The rules, however, make no allowances."

"Yes, sir. My question is—" He wasn't sure he wanted to ask it. But that medallion . . .

"Go ahead, please. What is your question?"

"Is it legal to kill your opponent in matches like this?"

"It happens, son," Kenyata said. "But that is not the objective today." Looking at Herdtmacher, he asked, *"Verstehen?"*

Both fighters answered. "Yes."

"Good." He handed each of them in turn a pen and the document. Both signed.

Herdtmacher said, "Herr Manley guarantees money. He hass not signed."

"His signature is not necessary yet, Expert Herdtmacher."

"Ah."

"Gentlemen, are you ready?"

So soon? John thought. Why so soon? But there was nothing left to do. The safe part of the match was over. He was afraid, and would have to fight that way. But just as that thought formed he felt that odd, cold serenity again. It wasn't complete, though; he merely felt it.

It seemed to be circling his mind like an airy cloud. He concentrated on needing it to come down, to wrap him like a blanket and to stay on him until this walking dream was over. And it came down, as he needed it.

John knew the crowd would be making noise now. Perhaps as much as before. But he didn't hear them. All he heard was his own heart, and the forceful pumping of air through his lungs. All he saw was the opponent. A body he needed to overcome, another person to conquer. He didn't know anymore why he needed to accept some pain and then pound this man into surrender. He just did, and so he was going to.

"Yes," John said.

"I also," the Duelist confirmed.

"Gentlemen. Begin!"

Something like cold air shot through John's brain, cool and focusing and anesthetic, and he was keenly ready. Pictures of a battle plan flashed behind his eyes. He "saw" Herdtmacher wait for his charge as before, then evade. But in reality the man closed in right away. The Duelist dropped to the dirt and rolled hard at his knees. John jumped forward instinctively and got his feet up barely in time. Herdtmacher rolled under him and leapt to his feet, poised and waiting. There was applause from the onlookers.

John feinted a grab at his opponent's legs. The Duelist responded with a straight-arm fist that felt like a boulder cracking his skull. The young giant reeled backward and watched, numb and detached, as the world lit up with brilliant explosions of light. His arms came open and spread like wings to catch his balance.

"No," Herdtmacher whispered, just loud enough to

be heard. "Trap too visible. You must come to me, Chon."

John stood still for a few seconds while the world stopped flashing. "Okay," he said.

The young giant roared and charged. In that instant an entire plan formed in his mind, clear as crystal. He raised his fists above his head to come down like sledgehammers on the Duelist's shoulders. It was another feint. He would stop at the last instant and take the man by the throat. Herdtmacher would hit him a few times and get away. But he could take the blows. He'd been horse-kicked often enough, and always walked away from it. If he could just squeeze for a second before Herdtmacher got away, it would be a fair trade. Then he'd do it all again. Herdtmacher wouldn't expect that. Two or three times would slow Herdtmacher considerably.

But the Duelist turned to his left and dropped low to the ground, spinning. He completed a circle with his left leg extended fully. It caught John just above the ankle and threw him into the air. He fell heavily on his back . . . landing with all the control and grace of a dead weight. This time he heard the crowd. They were screaming in ecstasy. Somehow he had landed directly on top of Thomas Klaus Herdtmacher.

John rolled off Herdtmacher and made a fast grab for his upper body. As the Duelist rolled in the other direction, John caught his right arm and dug in both thumbs with all his strength. It was like trying to crush stone. But it was flesh after all, and it gave way. Herdtmacher grunted in pain and after two attempts managed to jerk his arm free. He continued rolling to the edge of the circle and jumped to his feet. The crowd went into a frenzy.

Blood was seeping from two visible depressions on the Duelist's right biceps. Herdtmacher looked at the wound and then at his opponent. "Goodt hands, Chon." With a quick smile he shook his arm and walked back to the center of the combat circle.

The boy felt the excitement from the crowd as if it were a living thing inside him. It seemed to push out through his pores and give him strength at a level he'd never felt. He could win. He was going to win. This Duelist was just another body standing against him. It would yield eventually. That's how it had always been. And how it always would be.

Herdtmacher closed the distance slowly. John took a boxing stance and waited, bouncing on the balls of his feet. The spectators loved it. They were with him now, and he was with them. Not friends, but at least allies.

When the Duelist was a yard away something slammed into the right side of John's face. It stung like fire. He took a long step backward and was shaking his head to clear it, when it struck again in the same place. This time his head whipped violently to the left. He stepped back again and looked at Herdtmacher. He was sure the man hadn't moved. But in the back of his mind was a vague picture of something blurring at him from the Duelist's left side.

John brought his forearms closer in to his face and weaved from side to side. It came again. It didn't hurt as much this time. His face was numb and that cold serenity told him he was going to be all right. But his legs were shaking and bending at the knees, and he couldn't stop them. Not until he found himself kneeling in the dirt, unable to feel them. In a fraction of a second Herdtmacher was at his back, wrapping a stone-muscled left arm around John's neck. The young giant managed to get his chin down in time to protect his throat. But the pressure was relentless and irresistible. John's jaw was being crushed.

Herdtmacher whispered, "Iss time to rest in sefen seconds. Remember rest. Humility also. Iss important to fighter, yes?"

His legs were still numb, but John managed to lurch backward and get his feet beneath him. Pushing the much lighter man back should have been easy; as it was, lifting a cow would have been easier. Herdt-macher gave way slowly and John lunged suddenly for-ward, grasping Herdtmacher's arm and twisting as he dove for the ground. He landed on his back again, again on top of the Duelist. The neck-grip broke cleanly and John rolled away to his left. He was climbing to his feet when Kenyata called out, "Time!"

It took a few seconds for John to understand what the man was talking about. Time to rest, he remem-bered. Fifty seconds. He walked to the edge of the cir-cle and stepped out. The crowd closed in. He snarled at them like a mountaintooth. Someone yelled to give the boy some room.

John dropped to the ground and took several deep breaths. He'd survived two minutes and learned that Herdtmacher was a flesh-and-blood human being. That was a major thing to grasp, in all its meaning. The out-come was no longer a certainty, on either side. Sharp pain came to both his legs. Good, he could feel them again.

Looking across the circle, John saw Herdtmacher arguing with Muhammad Kenyata. They were both shouting in a language he had never heard. After a few seconds Kenyata turned away from the Duelist and strode angrily toward John.

He waved his hand. "No, don't get up. Rest while you can."

"What's wrong?"

"Thomas is being difficult. He's insisting that Mr. Manley sign the Fight Manifest before you continue."

"Why?"

The dark man sighed. "Wilfred Manley is his employer. The Fight Manifest is the document that binds him to pay Herdtmacher. It's legal proof that the match took place, once I sign it."

"I don't understand. Manley wouldn't dare refuse to pay him."

"I know that. But Thomas insists that it be done now. In practical terms it makes no difference. But technically, he's correct. It should have been signed before now."

"So what do we do?"

"I need your agreement to extend the rest period for three minutes. That will give Thomas time to go up there and get the damned thing signed."

"I have no objection, sir." Three minutes of additional rest sounded like a full night's sleep. John grinned. "You don't think Herdtmacher is tired, do you?"

Kenyata looked down at John. He seemed amazed at the question. "Son, I saw Thomas Herdtmacher fight and win eleven matches in one night, back on Earth. All were against established Duelists. The last two were death matches. Does that answer your question?"

John thought about that for a few seconds. "Was that a long time ago? When he was younger?"

"That was five weeks ago." He turned to go. "The three extra minutes start now. Good luck, son."

John watched as Kenyata crossed the circle and approached Herdtmacher. The fear was coming back, and the cold serenity was nowhere to be found. A thought occurred to him. Maybe that was the whole idea. Maybe Herdtmacher wanted him to get cold and stiff, and give him the time to think and become afraid again. Hell with that, he thought. He stood up and began stretching, then bouncing on his feet again. Let the Duelist think he was just getting started.

He watched as Herdtmacher took the manifest from Kenyata and walked to the first floor of the brothel. Herdtmacher called up to Manley in a voice too soft for John to hear. Manley said something in return and stood up. Herdtmacher waved a hand dismissively. He jumped for the edge of the floor above and swung up easily to stand next to Wilfred Manley. John noted that he'd done that little trick with just one arm. His left, the one that wasn't bleeding.

Manley was shaking his head. He seemed irritated by the delay. But he took the manifest and signed it. Herdtmacher took it back and bowed. He said something that made Manley laugh out loud and look down at John. The boy reddened and glared back.

Herdtmacher turned toward Iris in response to something she said and took a step backward into thin air. Manley reached for him as he began to fall. He missed, and Herdtmacher's face banged hard enough against the edge of the floor to be heard everywhere in the makeshift arena. The Duelist made a grab for the edge of the floor. He missed, too, and fell twelve feet to the ground below. He landed with a sickening thud.

John ran across the combat circle and pushed his way through the crowd to Herdtmacher. Kenyata yelled from behind him. "John, get back! Inside the circle!"

The boy looked back, confused. The old judge rushed past him. "Inside the circle! Now!"

John ran back to the center of the circle and waited. It seemed that half the spectators were trying to get to the Duelist, and the other half were shouting questions at John. He could only shrug his shoulders and wait, along with the rest of them.

The Peacekeepers pushed their way through and formed a human barrier around Kenyata and Herdtmacher. Manley was screaming incoherently from the floor above them.

Several minutes passed. The noise and shouted questions ebbed and flowed, with new rumors spreading every few seconds. Finally the protective ring of Peacekeepers parted. Two of them walked out with the Duelist between them. Each was supporting one of his shoulders. Herdtmacher's face showed no pain, only the impassive expression he'd worn before. But his left leg was bent backward at an obscene angle, at the knee.

The Peacekeepers half carried him to the combat circle. Kenyata followed close behind, waving at John to move away. In his hand was the Fight Manifest.

"It is my opinion," he called out over the murmuring. "It is my opinion that . . . Quiet!" The noise died immediately.

In the silence Herdtmacher said, "Herr Kenyata, I can continue match. Iss not bad inchury."

Kenyata snapped a reply in the strange language. The Duelist nodded and lowered his eyes.

The judge looked around in stony silence until not a sound could be heard from the spectators. "It is my judgment," he said, "that Thomas Klaus Herdtmacher is physically unable to continue in this combat. The match having legally begun, and . . . Quiet!" He waited again, his eyes sweeping the crowd. "The match having legally begun, and all governing rules having obtained, it is declared that the winner of this match is John Bi . . ."

"Wait!" John shouted. He looked around himself. Faces stared back. To some people he had occupied different roles in life. Grandson. Nephew. Friend. But there was no one present to claim any relation to him. Something about that, and what he knew Kenyata was about to say, bothered him. Finally it came to him. "I have no family name," he said firmly. "From this moment on it's John. That's all."

Kenyata looked at him curiously, then continued with his pronouncement. "It is declared that the winner . . ."

He heard the words. Felt them wash over him like startling, cool water. It was over. By the Blessed Saint Barrow, patron of all Duelists. Thomas Klaus Herdtmacher, Grade One Expert Duelist. Victor of three hundred fifteen death matches and thousands of nonlethal contests. Fell down. Fell off of floor. And shattered his leg.

It was absurd. It was the most ridiculous thing he'd ever heard.

Ko Kim would love it.

The young giant dropped to his knees. He raised

clenched fists to the skies above him and bellowed out deep things that swelled from the roots of his being. He went on, lost in it, until he was empty. And then, falling forward, he pounded his fists as hard as he could into the face of a world called Janus.

It was *over.*

The hard work, and the unspeakable joy of solitude, lasted for five days. On the sixth morning the first visitor to his cabin-in-the-making jumped from a flyer circling half a mile up in a cloudless sky. John identified the visitor through a new pair of binoculars and followed him down, watching as the chute popped open at six hundred feet. He winced just before the man hit the ground. But it was an easy landing in a patch of brown grass.

The visitor waved at the boy with one hand while releasing his harness with the other. "Hallo, Chon!"

Ten minutes later, within the four-foot walls that would soon be his kitchen, the two sat at a carved oak table. John poured two glasses of water. He shook his head, still stunned at the condition of his visitor. "No more jokes, please. Tell me *how* you did it."

Herdtmacher grinned. Today was the first time John had seen the man's real smile. It looked like a very natural expression for him. "Dobble-chointed," he said. "See?" He stood from the chair and indicated his left leg. With a *craaack* it bent backward at the knee, reaching an obscene angle.

The young giant winced. And then he sat silently, staring. Then he broke out laughing. It went on and on, until his aching stomach begged him to stop. He couldn't believe what this man, a stranger, had done for him. "But . . . why, Mr. Herdtmacher?"

"Herr Manley said you were trained, remember? Herr Manley lied to me. This iss not permitted to Expert Duelist." He smiled that wide, easy grin again. "Also, money iss same."

"But your reputation. Wasn't that . . . well, dishonest? Maybe?"

Herdtmacher shook his head. "Nein. Nefer dishonest. I did not claim inchury, remember? I said to Herr Kenyata I could continue in fight. Decission wass not mine to make."

John kept on staring. He was hesitant to keep questioning such incredible kindness. But what was this going to cost the Duelist? "Mr. Herdtmacher, you're famous on all the worlds. The media people told me about that. Won't word get around that you've broken your leg? How are you going to explain this? You won't be able to get any matches."

"Ah. But I haff fought three years with no rest. Now, I visit brother on Earth. I will rest."

"I remember what you whispered to me. Rest is important for a fighter."

"Chust so. Humility, also."

"So you slapped me a few times when I got cocky." John touched his face, which was still tender. *"Verstehen,"* he said. "I certainly do *verstehen.*"

"Goodt. You see, also, fighting iss goodt trade. Now you haff money for best furniture for house, best tools to build it."

"I couldn't believe it!" John said. "All those media people, they gave me money for my story!" He smiled and refilled the water glasses. "They were so generous,

I wanted to give them something a little more interesting than the truth. So I gave them all different stories. Pretty good ones, too. Now they've all got what they call "exclusive" stories to tell."

"Chust so!" Herdtmacher said, laughing. "Oh, I haff come to giff you this." He drew a thin book from a tunic pocket and handed it to John.

John looked at the book's cover. His eyes went wide.

"Iss about Admiral Simon Barrow," Herdtmacher said with a solemn air. "Also about Duelist school, Barrow Academy. My school. Best one."

"I . . . Thank you, Mr. Herdtmacher. Thank you. Do you think someday I might be good enough—"

"You can test on Landfall when you are sefenteen. If you are best of best, schools ask you to come. If you are best of best of best, Barrow Academy asks."

John's eyes shone. "After I've lived on it a year, this property becomes legally mine. I'll be able to sell it and pay for the school. If I make it."

Herdtmacher stood abruptly and offered his hand. "I will hear when you are testing. I will come, to watch you. Until again, Chon."

The boy escorted his guest through the gap that would soon be a doorway. He watched until Herdtmacher disappeared over the horizon in that strong, steady run. Portside was the nearest major shuttleport. By foot, the trip would take twenty days or more. But there was no hurry. Thomas Klaus Herdtmacher was resting.

That night he slept in his new bed for the first time, beneath a palette of stars. It was the most comfortable

sleep he'd ever had. The bed was just soft enough, and
more than big enough. There was even room for someone else. He hadn't seen Mary since before the fight.
He was sure she'd understand why he had needed time
alone. His life was different now, and he had needed
time to think about things.

But now he'd made up his mind.

First a visit to Gus and the twins, to see how they
were enjoying their new wealth. And then to Dennis
Town. He was too excited to eat breakfast. After
bathing at the newly dug well, he put on his new suit.
Also for the first time.

The tapestry, of the strange alien landscape that had always looked so cool and inviting, was gone. In its
place was old wallboard, unpainted. The door at the
end of the hallway was open. The small cluttered
kitchen where they'd sat and talked so many times was
empty.

Down the hall his former friend opened the door
from his study and stood silently watching as John
dropped an envelope on the floor. "It's what I owe you
for taking care of Gus and the twins," he said. "You can
use the rest to pay your gambling debts."

"John—"

"It's honest money. I just sold all the tools I bought
last week. Good-bye, Dr. Samuels."

"Can't you stay? A few minutes?"

"I've heard your story already. I talked with Mary
this morning."

"Then she told you—"

"Yes. She told me. I thought Manley had bribed one

or two of the other Council members. I wanted to believe that was all. I wasn't completely sure about you,
but I was never going to ask. And now . . . Mary's always told me the truth. This time I wish she hadn't."

"There was a reason."

"You took Manley's money because you want to go
home. Eusebeus is dying. Only a few people in Dennis
Town ever paid you, so you had almost no savings to
get home with. Too bad you bet it all on the fight."

"My family needs me, John. You can understand
that."

"So you risked mine, for a chance to help yours. Fair
enough." He turned to go.

"Are you going to Portside for the trial?"

John answered without turning. "I told the Peacekeepers everything I know. That's all the proof they
need. Besides, Mary says Iris confessed."

"She did. Manley paid her to do it. That was the first
part of his revenge against Gus. You were the second.
Now he's hiding somewhere."

"He's hiding in Hell. Good-bye."

"You're not going to look for him?"

"Why should I waste my time?"

After a few moments of silence Dr. Samuels said
from behind the young giant, "How *is* your family?
Gus, and your aunts?"

John wheeled around and glared with such force that
the young physician took a step backward. "I don't
know, Doctor. The house is empty. They're gone, and
so are the horses. They're rich now so they don't need
me. And that's the best news I got today." He felt like
a fool, for expecting to find them home. Maybe a thank
you, and he'd see they were all right, then go to town

to see Mary. There hadn't even been a note. They'd
have left before too long, anyway. With Wilfred Manley gone, Dennis Town would die. The citizens had cel-
ebrated his running off by destroying everything he'd
owned. The Pits, the mines, the farms, buildings, the
water treatment plant . . . all of it. There was no longer
any place to work. Everyone had hated Wilfred Manley. But they'd also depended on him for everything.
Including the character of the town. Now nothing was
left. If he ever stopped long enough to think about it, he
might try to give a damn.

"Good-bye, John. I hope you can forgive me. For
your sake, not mine."

"I wished Mary a happy life with you. I wish you the
same. For her sake, not yours. But if you ever hurt
her . . ." He clenched his hands and made himself open
them again.

"She offered me the money she'd saved, John. The
same way she offered it to you. I didn't ask her for it."

"Good-bye, Doctor."

Gus and the twins had abandoned the old flyer. It was
the last thing John had to sell when he reached Portside. The dealer cheated him, and he didn't care. The
money was enough for some new rough-around
clothes, a few days' food, and the first payment for Ko
Kim's new eyes. That was all he wanted. He could
sleep in the parks until he found work.

The walk to the hospital took two hours. Portside
was a lot bigger, without a flyer. One of the elevators
was out of service and the other two were packed with
employees reporting for the afternoon shift. The stairs

were quicker, anyway. He ran up to the nineteenth floor and asked for Ko Kim's room. The nurse gave him a frightened stare, and a number.

The room was a jumble of cleaning tools, rags, and buckets. Boxes of supplies were lined up against three of the walls. Space had been cleared for a bed, but the bed was empty. John walked back out in the corridor and was met by a small woman in a nurse's uniform. "I know who you must be," she said. "Let me take you to the doctor on duty."

The young nurse sat quietly, holding his hand, while he absorbed the news.

"I'm very sorry, Mr. ah, John." The surgeon was a thin middle-aged man who held a folder and scratched his chin as he spoke. "We couldn't stop the virus. It says in here you were informed that we wouldn't be able to. All we could do was monitor her, and try to make her comfortable."

"Yes."

"Then this isn't a grievance?"

"No."

"Good. Let's see then, time of death . . . yesterday, at four-twenty-two." He looked up at John. "I'm sorry I wasn't more involved with this case. Fascinating pathology. Quite unique, in terms of—"

The nurse stood up. "Doctor! This boy is—"

"That's all right," John said. "Was there any pain?"

The surgeon shook his head. "I doubt it. But as I was about to say, the woman . . ." He opened the folder again and scratched his chin. "Yes, Ko Kim. Apparently she had an episode of lucidity just minutes before she expired. It lasted only a few seconds, but considering the massive damage to her brain tissue, that was quite remarkable."

"What does 'lucidity' mean?"

"She spoke. Astonishing, isn't it?" He stood up and closed the folder, preparing to leave.

"What did she say?"

"I don't know, young man. I have many patients to attend to, and can't be everywhere at once. The point is, she spoke. That should not have been possible."

"Maybe it's written there on her chart," the nurse suggested.

"Yes, perhaps it is." The surgeon sat down again with a hard glance at the nurse. He opened the folder and scanned the pages. "Yes, here it is. Gibberish. Perhaps another language. But at the end she seemed to be asking for her brother, named John."

The young giant looked into the two pair of eyes watching him. The money in his pocket wouldn't help Sister Kim. But it would buy a ticket on the first off-world shuttle leaving Janus. He exhaled slowly and put his head back, focusing on the ceiling. He willed it to disappear. The ceiling yielded and gave way, and then the planet itself faded within his mind to a stark nothingness. And he saw for the first time the eight hundred worlds, the Great Domain, that lay beyond. It was Sister Kim's parting gift.

"That's right," he said. "She was calling to me, by the only name I have. I'm Brother John."

II LANDFALL

A Duelist showed up as John and the others were loading onto the shuttle. *DOMA* was a gargantuan liner and on that morning there would be fifty shuttles loading at nine different bays. Theirs were the first to load from Bay C23. John had seen the Duelist once before, in transit, and knew that her name was Marnie—something. She was about as friendly as anyone could be, passing through the group of eighty and stopping here and there to shake a hand, ask a name, wish good luck. That sort of thing. When she got to John she stared. But not like most people do. This was professional. Not, "How big *is* this guy," but more like, "If I had to kill him, where would I start?" John appreciated the difference. Marnie was a Duelist. He wanted to learn how to think like one.

John was hoping she'd say something to him, something professional. But she just stared for a few seconds and moved on. That could have been because John was staring back at her for reasons that weren't entirely professional; along with being a certified killing machine, Marnie was also extraordinarily beautiful.

The distribution of candidates was eighty per shuttle. After John's group lined up and was ready to board, Marnie jumped up on a little platform, graceful and easy, and addressed the whole group. "You are about to begin three of the most important days you will ever live. Remember how hard you've already worked to get to Landfall. Obey every order you're given. Don't listen to rumors. Don't start any. Remember why you're here . . ." She went on for a few more minutes, putting sentences together in no particular order, but making a lot of sense in all. At the end she said, "This is your first order. As soon as you're in the shuttle's hold, find a place and sit comfortably. During your brief ride down to the planet you are not to move around. That's all. Go aboard now, and good luck."

That was a joke. The cargo hold was bare metal. No seats, no straps. It was big enough to squeeze in, maybe, sixty or so people if they stood up and squeezed together. Now eighty people had been ordered to sit down—comfortably. Because of John's size and grave countenance he was given plenty of room by the others, who made stacks of dangling or twined limbs and squeezed bodies. Only one candidate dared to invade his space. That was how John first met Linda Doya. She pushed her back up against his and said to no one in particular, "My mattress at home is like your back. Warm, hard, and wide."

She opened a dialogue by jabbing her elbow into John's left kidney. After the third or fourth time he asked, "Am I bothering you?"

"No, that's okay. I just wondered if you'd feel that."

"Yes," he said. "I do."

"Well, that's a good sign. We can be friends if you want."

"Why?"

"Because I'm smarter than anybody here, that's why. And I guess you already know what you are."

The "brief ride" joke stretched into its sixth hour and the "comfortably" part of the beautiful Duelist's humor was wearing thin by now. The fellow to John's right had long skinny legs and had made the mistake of being too polite. To make room for the others he'd sat with his heels tucked up against his butt, with half of two different people on top of him, and he was in misery after the first hour. But he didn't move except to scratch at his knees every few minutes. That couldn't have helped. John guessed it was a body language way of telling his legs he was doing something for them, and to quit complaining.

The kid sitting face-to-face with Long-legs said this was his second tryout on Landfall and it was the same last time. They were being tested, he said. He explained that no Duel School was going to recruit someone who couldn't obey a simple order or who'd whine about little things like screaming cramps and howling pain. His name was Lobo Sparinada, and he claimed to remember three or four candidates or his last trip who just disappeared as soon as the shuttle landed. Why? Well, he said, who was he to say? Maybe they had moved, or complained. He didn't want to start any rumors.

"They were monitoring you?" Long-legs asked. His name was Keith Joycel.

Sparinada was a pleasant-enough-looking kid, with

olive skin and a round face like a baby's. But when he
stared the way he did at Joycel, he looked about as
friendly as death. His black eyes were hard as obsidian
daggers. "Yes," he said, "if I have to say so directly. We
were being watched. Just like we are now. That's what
I'm explaining. Is it clear now?"

Joycel glared back at him and tensed. Cramps or not,
if he could work a body part loose he was ready to
swing it at Lobo.

But Sparinada gave him a sweet smile. A smile like
that shouldn't have been able to sit on the same face as
that knife-edged stare, but it did. "Good," he said.
"Sometimes I'm not very good at explaining things. It's
embarrassing."

Joycel thought that over and smiled back at him.
"You did fine," he said. "We're all grateful."

"Oh, he's a treasure," someone said from the meat-
pile. "We'll never make it without him."

Sparinada had no one on top of him and he made as
if to leap to his feet, but didn't. He just twisted his neck
around in search of whoever had made the remark.
John made up his mind about Lobo Sparinada right
then: He was a damned good actor, to switch expres-
sions so fast, or he was a crazy person. Either way, he
was someone who needed a behind-the-back kind of
watching. John remembered seeing him around on
DOMA, usually keeping to himself, but he didn't remember hearing anything about Sparinada being at
Landfall before. That's something that would have gotten around quickly. So John marked him as a liar, too,
trying to make himself important to the shuttle group.
As it turned out later he wasn't entirely right or entirely
wrong.

Deciding to tune out Sparinada, John turned his attention to two voices coming from the far side of the compartment. The first was male, and the second female.

"Hackin' garbage scow! You should see this compartment. Both engines are out now!"

"We've landed, okay? Stop complaining."

"We didn't land, Sweetums Lady. It was a fall. We plummeted. Dropped. You broke every hackin' thing that was strung together down here. Now pipe me some hackin' oxygen!"

"How about a hackin' divorce, instead?"

"You decide, Sweetums Lady. You're the captain, remember?"

His height gave him a good view. The voices were so distinctive it would have taken a while to convince anyone that both of them were coming from the same person. Or to explain why there was applause going on. So he didn't try; he just listened with everyone else.

"Those were the first words ever spoken on Landfall," the speaker was saying in a third voice. This one sounded as natural as the first two. He was a boy of about twenty. Because no one got this far in the Duelist selection process without being some kind of spectacular athlete, John couldn't help wondering how he handled all the extra weight he carried around on his short frame. He was like a pink-faced statue of Buddha with big round blue eyes and a long curly gold wig.

"The words were spoken in the Domain Standard

year of 2221," Golden Head went on, "by William J.
Lockhart, a third-rate engineer and first-rate whiner, and
his wife, Constance J. Lockhart." Every other conversation in that cargo hold stopped. The kid had everyone's
attention now. "Constance was pilot, owner, and master
of the vessel *NADEEN*. In an era characterized by people exactly like themselves, the Lockharts were dream-
ers, long on ambition and short on know-how. Progress
and growth in Great Domain did not always follow an
orderly path."

"Is this a true story?" someone asked.

"Shhh!" That was from at least ten people.

The chubby kid's talent for drama had made the
group forget their discomfort, and he had all of them
wrapped up in the various voices. It was like God had
pulled a few people aside to tell them a story, before He
went back to being Himself. They all felt privileged.

"Their words might seem ungrateful," the kid went
on, "given the fact that Constance and William were
saved from certain death by the planet's unexpected
presence in a region of space containing nothing else
even remotely comforting. Not to two lost pioneers
desperately short of food, air, and patience. And especially, aboard a craft whose previous owners had been
masters of deceit and servants to no recognizable sense
of decency. *NADEEN* was not a garbage scow. It could
never have qualified for the job.

"But whether or not the words were ungrateful, they
are recorded facts. And prophetic. Twenty-eight years
after they were uttered, that's thirty-eight years ago, a
bona fide exploration team arrived. The team discov-
ered, not far from where we will land, a ramshackle ship
torn apart to provide two sets of living accommoda-

tions. These accommodations could easily have been
built with materials readily available in nearby forests.
But they ripped the ship apart instead. There were no
working communication devices of any kind, except for
the tape of that one conversation. But there were two diaries, each covering twenty-three years on Landfall.
These were almost illegible. Inarticulate. But in their
ways they were masterpieces of fear, frustration, loneli-
ness, isolation, accusations, bitterness, hatred, and at
last, fantasies of murder in its grisliest forms. The team
also found two corpses. Both asphyxiated. His, a murder. Hers, a suicide. But listen to this, friends. The
deaths occurred twenty-three years apart."

"How can that be, if both diaries were the same time
frame and—"

"Shhh!"

"After the bodies were duly interred, Private-Major
Glenn Avery Charles of the Exploration Service reread
NADEEN's logs and played the landing tape again. He
filed the standard paperwork and then he took a walk in
a bright sun-kissed valley where he had a long, deep
think. Private-Major Charles was a contemplative man,
you see, who looked for the moral point in any situation. As he saw it, William was at fault."

"What do you mean? She killed him!" someone
said.

"Murdered him," someone added.

The kid didn't break his rhythm. "At the worst possible moment, William forced Constance to weigh his
years of whining and accusations against the value of
precious ship's air. Remember, he demanded some
oxygen. She couldn't have been certain yet that the
world had a lovely, rich atmosphere. So she kept the air

and gave him the divorce. What Private-Major Charles perceived, you see, was a Captain's prerogative combined with a wife's cry for relief. And then poor Constance paid for her decision. Very horribly. With twenty-three years of emotional agony that you and I cannot even imagine. You see, from the day of their landing onward, from the day she killed her husband, she lived William's life as well as her own. Constance became husband and wife, whiner and stoic, male and female, incompetent engineer and incompetent commander, each manifestation harboring a bottomless wellspring of pure malice in and for the other. She kept both diaries. She was a person cleft in twain by guilt."

"Cleft in what?"

"It means cut in two pieces," Linda called out. "Now shut up."

"Oh."

"One body," Golden Head continued. "Bearing two souls locked in unremitting hatred and warfare. Such was the existence of that poor creature, for as long as she could bear the paradise of Eden."

Then minutes of silence. People jabbed one another for breathing too loudly.

Golden Head had more to say. "Private-Major Charles returned from his sojourn in that sun-kissed valley in a satisfied state of mind. For he was a man who loved a good human tragedy. Now, don't mistake me. Private-Major Charles was as compassionate as each of you. But he believed that all great events require human tragedy as fuel. Can any historian argue? Or philosopher? And so he rejoiced, for the riches he could claim as the world's true discoverer. For the birth of a new home for humankind. A home whose mortgage, shall we say, had been paid in advance and in full by the Lockharts. One piece of this bizarre episode, though, he found very amusing. It was on the tape. 'We didn't land . . . It was a *fall*.'"

"Landfall! I get it!"

"Will you shut *up?*"

"Thus"—from Golden Head—"the name of the planet below.

"Now, I ask you to put it all together, and consider with me. Consider how Fate directs the lives that we mortals enjoy. For I say to you, and no proof can be more irrefutable, that Fate is not blind. Nor cruel. Nor capricious. She is, my colleagues, a poet."

There wasn't a sound in that hold for a long minute. But Golden Head wasn't quite finished.

"Landfall is now in legal limbo," he continued. "It will remain so until the year 2321, which is the century anniversary of its discovery. That is, if no heir of the Lockharts steps forward to claim it. In the meantime it is used by the powerful and well-connected Duelist Union as a place to test prospective students like us. Fitting, isn't it? The Lockharts are now tucked away on the back shelves of memory, along with other obscurities of history. But their legacy looms below us at this moment. This world known as Landfall was born in, and in its service to humankind has come to symbolize, one word: contention. Do you understand? Some of us will emerge from the experience of Landfall as Private-Major Charles did: with the opportunity to become new, freshly made creatures. Destiny's Children, as Duelists were once called. With life an open carnival, and you on the midway. With a fierce thirst for adventure, and untold riches to spend. But others of you, in

fact most of you who are here, will emerge as Constance Lockhart did. Broken in spirit and body. Endur-
ing the remainder of your lives in a state of hopeless
disgrace. Haunted, made grotesque, barely human . . .
by a moment's weakness that you will never forget and
never escape. And some of you . . . some of you will
suffer William's fate. You will not emerge at all. Your
lives are ending now, at this moment. Some of you
have seen the last familiar, loving face you will ever
see. You have tasted your last breath of happiness." A
long pause, and then, "Thus, Landfall. And welcome."

Something was said then that I couldn't make out,
but I heard Golden Head's answer. This was in a fourth
voice that turned out to be his usual one. "I know the
complete story because of who I am. My name is Glenn
Avery Charles. The Third."

That brought a mix of voices, and a snort from Linda
Doya.

"Now *there's* something!" someone called out.

"Sure is," someone else said. "I've heard of Private-
Major Charles."

"So have I. He was famous."

"Have you now?" Glenn Charles asked. "Well,
there's more. As I have told you, Private-Major Charles
is recorded as the true discoverer of this world. And so
if none of the Lockhart descendants show up by the
century anniversary of Landfall's discovery, I will
come to own a good piece of this planet. The Exploration Service will claim fifty-one percent and turn it to
public use for all citizens of the Great Domain. But the
rest is mine, as sole heir to Private-Major Charles.
Who, as a *Private*-Major, meaning that he capitalized
the expedition with his own funds, thus assuming the

monetary risks of failure, thus allowing the Service to multiply its efforts exponentially, is entitled to prize money. Or raw land, in this case."

"Say . . ."

"I wondered what a Private-Major was."

"That's because you're ignorant. Isn't that right, Mr. Charles?"

"We'll look out for you, Mr. Charles."

"Please," Glenn Charles answered. "Don't bother. And I'd better not catch any one of you sneaking over to my property. Not unless you go to the same Duelist school I do. And graduate. And make something of your miserable, gullible lives. Because," he said, going back to that narrative voice, "Glenn Avery Charles the First was a Peacekeeper lieutenant who never left the soil of his native world. And whose only contribution to the Great Domain was in siring my father. Landfall is called Landfall because Landfall is the planet's name."

Then, he crossed his ankles under his crotch, put his hands palm-up on his knees, and closed his eyes. The trainee Duelists erupted, to the extent their confined space allowed. Charles had swept them up in a kind of magic spell, and then he'd let them down hard. Some fell away angry, and others hit the ground, laughing. Glenn Charles had found a way to get comfortable and no one made a move to punish him.

"You believed him, didn't you? Ha!"

"Well, *you* said you knew who Private-Major Charles was!"

"I was just helping him fool you idiots."

"Who are you calling idiots?"

It went on, building every second.

The shuttle pilot must have thought there was a riot in progress. There might have been one, with some attacking and some defending Glenn Charles, and John felt sure he wouldn't have even twitched, no matter how close the fight got to him. But just then the shuttle landed, actually bouncing a couple of times. It was more like a fall.

Linda Doya was the first to her feet. She was a tiny woman with skin as dark and pure as space. "You'd better stay near me," she told John. "I've got something important to tell you about that Charles boy."

The hatchway leading out from the cargo hold popped open as soon as the shuttle stopped. Just about everyone decided this was the time to groan about being cramped for so long. There was pushing and snarling, untangling of limbs, and a lot of laughing. Lobo Sparinada was the last one up. "Don't be in such a hurry," he said. He was nearly trampled before he could tell them why. Keith Joycel's knees popped like toy cannons when he stood up. Glenn Charles pushed through the pack of bodies, and was one of the first to reach the exit hatch.

They assembled outside in blinding sunlight and waited for someone to appear with instructions. Linda Doya was practically attached to John's leg by then. "That's right," she said. "Stay close."

John had been hoping to see Marnie-something again, but no one was there.

The shuttle started to lift off while the last five were still in the doorway, and they had to jump for it. All of them hit the ground from fifteen feet in the air, rolled, and got to their feet. There was a lot of applause. They bowed and smiled and went around shaking hands, like real Duelists after a match. John felt a chill. Seeing those five kids act like Duelists reminded him that eighty percent of the group was guaranteed to be rejected. That also meant that twenty percent would make it to one of the twelve Duel Schools, but his mind wasn't up to looking on the bright side just then.

The shuttle took only seconds to get out of sight, headed back to *DOMA*. The group was left standing in a field of grass beneath a clear blue sky. In every direction, about fifty yards away, was thick woods. There were no other groups of candidates, or shuttles, to be seen. The sun was directly overhead.

"What now? someone asked.

The answer that came was, "I don't know. Ask Lobo."

Sparinada didn't know at first he was being made fun of. He said everyone should be patient and wait. "After this thing starts, you'll all wish you were back here wondering what comes next."

"Why should we have to wonder? We've got you to tell us."

"Just be patient. It's probably different for every group."

"I guess that makes you pretty useless, doesn't it?" It was the same male voice that had referred to him as a "treasure" before.

Lobo took a running dive over a line of people to get at that taunting voice. He came back into view, dragging a young man by the feet. The kid was holding his stomach and laughing so hard he was helpless for the half minute it took Lobo to drag him to the center of a circle they'd accidentally formed when they first assembled. Real excitement passed through the group. A combat circle! It was easy to imagine Lobo and that kid as two Duelists getting ready for a death match. The fact that one was dragging the other, who was laughing like a maniac, didn't make any difference at the time.

John expected them to stop and stand face-to-face. Then Lobo would announce to the crowd that he'd been insulted to a point beyond what a Duelist could accept. But as a good Duelist he was ready, even eager, to forgive the insult in exchange for an apology. The kid of course would refuse, politely, because Duelists do not apologize. (So everyone thought.) Lobo would then challenge him. The kid would nod and recite the traditional, "Since it must be so." Then someone would shout, "Commence!" and the fight would be on.

That wasn't what happened. When Lobo let go of the kid's feet, the kid spun around on his butt, got his feet under him, and pushed off backward from the ground, straight at Lobo. His back slammed into Lobo's chest and lifted him. The kid jammed his feet down, reached between his own legs, and snatched up Lobo's ankles as they were rising, jerked him flat on his back to the ground, pulled him out between his own legs, and sat, hard, on his stomach, still holding Lobo's ankles. That blew all of Lobo's air out. The whole thing was over in seconds. Then the kid got up. "You probably deserve better than that," he said, addressing Lobo Sparinada. "And I'll be proud to count you as a friend if you'll understand my position. You see, I can't be treated in that way, because it wasn't me you had reason to go after. My name is Ben Slate."

Why had he been laughing? As Ben explained it to

John much later, "Sparinada could have released me any time prior to our arrival in that ring, and because I was laughing I could have behaved as if I were part of a joke. But as soon as we entered that ring, everything changed. At that moment it became an insult, and serious enough to warrant the ridiculous way I put him on the ground."

Lobo took quite a few shallow breaths before trying a deep one. When he could breathe, he said, "It wasn't you?"

"No."

Lobo stretched out his hand, and Ben helped him up. "All right. No offense taken, then," Lobo said, which was only half of what he should have said. Ben Slate nodded to him and walked back into the crowd.

Linda Doya gave John a sharp elbow in the hip. "Never mind the jumping," she told him. "That was just show. But did you see his hands? No, you didn't, because I almost didn't. He's a genius with them. I know that hold he had on Lobo's ankles. He could have paralyzed him with pain. It took him about a tenth of a second to get that hold and it was perfect from the time he got it. Did you notice he never shifted his hands? Not even a little? You've got to learn to see these things. That boy will make it to Barrow Academy, and he'll be an Empty-hand."

John stared down at her as if she'd just sprouted a couple of extra arms. She was describing the elite of the elite. Empty-hand specialists would fight against any weapon, any armor. Usually they were dressed in a loincloth, and they never used anything more than what the name suggested. It was what's known as a "thin" specialty, in this case because very few Duelists lasted more than a month or two after announcing their intent. The others either came to their senses and recanted, or succeeded for a while and then were hacked to pieces.

"Let me help you picture what I'm saying," Linda said. "A Twoyard sword is another thin specialty because it's so difficult to master. The sword weighs eighty-five pounds. By the time you're certified with it as a Grade Five Journeyman Duelist, you'll stand with the weapon sheathed at the center of a ten-foot radius circle. There will be nine slender poles and one thick one, all ten feet tall, within or at the border of that circle. There's a peach or an apple impaled on the thin poles at different heights, from six inches to ten feet off the ground. Someone shouts, "Commence!" You draw the Twoyard and begin cutting into each piece of fruit. The poles they're impaled on can't be touched. One pole is solid oak and a foot thick, and you've got to cleave through that with one pass. You have eight seconds to complete the test. Now picture this: You have a laser-honed Twoyard in one hand, full body armor, and a face that would turn a rabid mountaintooth to jelly. That boy, that Empty-hand, is dressed in a loincloth and armed with all the air he can hold in his hands. He's got to overcome you, kill you, or die. "Commence!"

At that time no school but Barrow Academy had ever produced a successful Empty-hand, and the other Duel Schools were desperate to know Barrow's training secrets. This is what Linda Doya was saying about a kid she'd never seen before the shuttle ride.

"Maybe he'd better stay close to you too," John suggested. "You can watch out for those hands he's a genius with."

"He will," she said. "The three of us will be insepa-rable by the time we graduate from Barrow."

Fortunately for John, his stunned silence was inter-rupted before it became embarrassing.

"Shut up!"

The voice came from the forest that surrounded them. From which direction, it was impossible to tell. Fifty or so candidates were pointing in as many differ-ent directions.

"The sign-up desk is six miles north. You have one hour to get there."

"Which way is north?" was asked by so many of us at once, it sounded like one voice.

"Shut up!"

Lobo Sparinada got a smile on his face and took off in a dead run, pumping his arms ahead of him. He cov-ered the clearing fast and disappeared into the woods. A crowd followed him, flowing like an amoeba going after food. A few stayed where they were.

"Test question," Linda Doya said John. "Why aren't we running?"

"I'm not running because that Lobo kid doesn't know any more than the rest of us do," he said. "What about you?"

"Him," she said. She pointed to Glenn Charles, who was sitting like the Buddha again. "If we had to go somewhere, he'd already be there. Which means that he is. Which means that we are, too."

"Then why ask me?"

"A test, like I said. See? The Empty-hand didn't run off either. And there's Mark Tannen and Roy Billsworth, and I don't know the other six."

"You seem to be saying that Glenn Charles is the smartest one among us. I thought that was you."

"He's only smart for himself. I'm smart for a lot of people at once."

She seemed satisfied that the different forms of smartness spoke for themselves. All John understood from the exchange was that Linda Doya wasn't going to be pinned with words. He followed her a few yards to where Charles sat. "What's going on?" she asked him.

He looked up at her, taking his time. His head cranked up as if it were mounted on a slow swivel. "You're from Hadrian, aren't you?"

"The crown jewel of the Sewer System," she said.

Glenn Charles laughed and looked up at John. The swivel didn't seem to want to go that high. "She means the Magus Solar System," he said. "It's a nickname. A joke."

"Thanks," John said. Not everyone believed, but most seemed to, that being huge meant being stupid. He'd had time to get used to that.

The swivel cranked slowly down to Linda's level. "So you know."

"That's right. I never missed an episode. Or a lecture."

Glenn Charles took in a deep breath and let it out through his nose. "We eighty are from one shuttle. There are forty-nine others like it from *DOMA*. And there are fifty similar shuttles from each of eleven other utility liners just like *DOMA*. That makes us forty-eight thousand in all, arriving this day on Landfall, representing all of the eight hundred sixty worlds of the

Great Domain. We are 68 percent male, 32 percent female, average age 19.6 years."

Linda Doya nodded at him. "That's what I thought."

John didn't like how it looked, at his size, following a woman who barely topped his waist. But he did follow, like a puppy waiting for the next scrap. "Well?" he asked after they'd moved away from Glenn Charles.

"Weren't you listening?"

"I didn't miss a single statistic. What I missed is the reason we're staying here." And suddenly he got it. "There are forty-eight thousand of us in all, and only one Duelist camp. They wouldn't spread us out too far. So there must be dozens of groups of candidates in clearings like this one, all over these woods. Picture the forest like a big sheet of dough with six hundred biscuit holes cut out."

"That'll work."

"And those other groups, at least the closer ones, would all hear the same announcement. So how can there possibly be one sign-up desk? We'd all be here through next week, just signing in."

"Right. And that great mysterious voice said it's six miles north. But north of what?"

"Maybe it, if there is an 'it,' is about six miles north of a point that's about six miles south of us."

"Exactly."

"Okay, exactly six miles."

Linda looked proud of him, but she didn't get his joke. John already had decided she was a valuable friend, and maybe they really would become unseparable, but it was a shame about her sense of humor.

A group of young people, strangers, broke from the line of trees behind Linda, and within a few seconds she and John were surrounded. John counted fifteen of them, silent and hard-faced.

Finally one of them spoke. He was a rail-thin kid of about eighteen with close-cropped red hair and freckles. "We're tired of this," he said. His voice was deep and melodic, like that of a trained singer. "There's no answer to this puzzle except maybe to beat it out of you. That's it, right? We have to beat it out of real Duelists? Well, that's what we're going to do. So get ready."

"What are you talking about?" Linda asked. The kid charged at her. He was bent at the waist, with his arms outstretched. Linda left the ground and dove at him, high, as if she were doing a jackknife into a lake. His arms closed together where her feet had just been. By then she had caught his shoulders and used him like a springboard. She went into a somersault while he passed beneath her. She landed squarely on her feet and whirled around to face him. "Ya-*ha!*" she said.

The boy's momentum carried him headfirst into John's lower abdomen. John lifted him by the collar and held him dangling at arm's length "What was that?" he asked. What the boy had done was too lame to be an attack, and too hostile to be anything else.

By way of answering, the redhead screamed, "I'm not afraid of you!" He cut the air with his fists, missing John by more than a foot. "All I want is a fair chance," he said. Now he was whining, which was embarrassing. "You can't disqualify me over some stupid puzzle!" His face turned so red his freckles disappeared.

The kid's companions were looking from him to John, and then to each other. Two of them, a boy and a girl who looked a lot alike, stepped inside the circle

formed by the others. They took a few deep breaths and
lowered their shoulders for a charge.

"Wait a minute," John said. He let go of the red-
faced kid, who had embarrassed himself enough for
one day. He caught his balance and backed away to
stand with the other two. They were getting their
courage together when John said, "You win. We surrender."

"You do?" the girl asked.

"We do," Linda said. She had the biggest grin on her
face. "You're not from our shuttle, are you?"

"I knew it!" Red-face kicked at the grass and looked
down like he was searching for a big stick. "You two
were the pilots! Well, now you're going to answer for
that ride!"

About this time the kid who'd humiliated Lobo
Sparinada, the one Linda had christened "Empty-
hand," walked into the circle. In the silence John noticed his eyebrows, steel gray and bushy, like
caterpillars meeting in the middle of his forehead. "I'm
the sign-up warden," he announced to the new arrivals.
"My name is Benjamin Slate. Is there a problem?"

"Finally!" Red-face cried out.

John was as relieved as Red-face was. All this time,
he thought, we've had a real Duelist among us. Ben
Slate looked no more than seventeen, but who was to
say? Linda put an end to that idea. "You're not helping," she said to Slate. "These people are frightened
and lost."

Ben Slate's skin was nearly as dark as Linda's, so he
must have blushed pretty hard for John to see it from
fifteen feet away.

"We're not Duelists, or pilots," Linda said to Red-

face and the look-alikes standing with him. "But thanks
for thinking we were. We're just candidates, like you."

"Then where are we supposed to go?" the girl asked.
She gave Benjamin Slate a nasty look. He shrugged his
shoulders and grinned like a first-class rogue in the
holo's. The picture of innocent mischief. She smiled
back. That told John a lot about Ben Slate, and all of it
would turn out to be correct.

"I don't think we need to go anywhere," Linda told
her. She cited Glenn Charles's statistics and her analy-
sis of what they meant. She even gave John credit for
helping to figure it out. That seemed to satisfy the newcomers, or else they were too tired and frustrated to
argue. It turned out they were from different shuttles,
some of them from three or four miles away, although
they admitted it was hard to judge. There were groups
like this spread out everywhere. The look-alikes estimated that they'd been here for more than ten hours.
That made them old-timers.

"Shut up!"

That voice again. Comforting and infuriating.

*"If you are in a clearing, remain where you are. If
you are in the woods, proceed to the nearest clearing.
This is now your primary group. One of you from each
primary group will make a list of all your names,
worlds of origin, and Standard birth dates. The lists
will be collected shortly. Any individual not registered
in a primary group is rejected. Any group not produc-
ing a list when required is rejected, one and all. The
rest of you, don't pity them. They're getting out easy.
Most of you will be badly injured and humiliated before
we allow you to leave."* The speaker clicked off, then
on again. *"Oh. And we expect two hundred forty of you*

*to die while you're visiting us. Don't disappoint us,
children."*

"Well," Glenn Charles remarked. He was there
again, sitting with his arms folded over his belly. John
still had never seen him walk. "A comforting statistic.
One half of one percent isn't bad, is it? With twenty-
seven in our group, that means that just over one-tenth
of one of us has to die. Losing a finger and a couple of
toes should satisfy the requirement. That will leave the
rest of us statistically safe from bodily harm. Volun-
teers?"

The newcomers didn't know what to make of
Charles. Not that John did, either. He wasn't surprised
that Linda Doya had two pens and several sheets of
paper folded up in a sleeve-pocket. She had everyone
line up and pass by her, and made the list.

About fifteen minutes later a shuttle almost touched
down in the clearing. As it hovered about ten feet off
the ground. A woman jumped down to the grass and
started counting. "Ten . . . nine . . . eight . . ." It was
that beautiful Duelist again, Marnie-something.

Glenn Charles flashed by Linda, snatched the list,
and delivered it to Marnie at the count of three. Those
fat legs could move in a blur. He and Marnie exchanged a couple of words, and she retreated back into
the shuttle by leaping for the bottom of the access,
catching it, and swinging herself aboard as neatly as
you could ask. The move was so similar to the acrobat-
ics of Thomas Klaus Herdtmacher, Grade One Expert
Duelist, that John felt a hive of bees wake up and go to
war in his stomach. Five years had passed since Herdtmacher had said he would be here when John tested.
The fear of disappointing Herdtmacher gave every one

of those bees an extra stinger. The shuttle flew off as silently as it had arrived.

"She will be permitted into my kingdom," Charles announced to no one in particular when he got back to the group. "She is a Bellenauer Belle, as I suspected."

"What kingdom?" Roy Billsworth said. He looked quick enough, and mean enough, and clever enough, to make a living pulling the wings off flies. "That was all a lie."

"I'm afraid it was the lie that was the lie," Glenn Charles told him, and shrugged. "As lies go, what can be better? And if they don't, what does it matter?"

If there was a parade for people who can look mean and stupid at the same time, Roy Billsworth's expression would have earned him a place in the front. Not that John didn't have the same questions he did. But John wasn't stupid enough to ask them. "What does that mean?" Billsworth asked.

Glenn Charles must have felt pity for him. "Word will pass soon enough, so there is no point in denying it further," he said. "I am heir to the world you see before you."

"Translation?" Billsworth's friend, Mark Tannen, asked. His was a face and build that could blend into any crowd and disappear.

"I suppose I have to tell the story," Linda said. "Although he's pretending he doesn't want me to. Back on Hadrian there's a holo series that's been running for years. It's pretty good, I think. Funny, and a lot of real history. Called The Fighting Lockharts. Every episode starts and ends with a narrator. He's an actor, playing the man who found their logs after they were dead. Private-Major Glenn Avery Charles."

"So it's all true," John said.

Linda gave him a look. She was disappointed that he'd say something so obvious. But then she smiled because it gave her a way to end the story. "It isn't *all* true," she said. "The series is fiction mixed with fact. But a lot of it's true, like the pictures of the real Lockharts they show at the end, along with the real Private-Major Charles. He used to visit Hadrian and lecture before he died. He was almost as big a celebrity at home as the actor who played him. Glenn Avery Charles the Second took over for him, and he used to drag his little boy along on his lectures. So I know who this is. We've met."

"We were children then," Charles said.

"I hope you've learned to keep your hands off other children," Linda said. "Especially off little girls who can punch."

"I never repeat a mistake," he said.

"Well, that's good."

"And by the way, that humiliating incident inspired me to become the fighter I am today. And will be."

"You too?" Linda gave him a friendly laugh. It wasn't until John noticed her body relaxing just then that he was aware of how tensed up she'd been. "I always wished I could have hit you harder. Now I can."

Glenn Charles could smile, too. "We'll discuss the matter after we've both graduated. For now, perhaps a mutual thank you is in order."

"I'll take an apology first."

"You have it. Along with my thanks."

Doya looked up at John as if she'd just dragged out the biggest deer in the forest and spitted it over the fire. "That's good enough for me," she said. "You?"

"Good enough," John said. It should have seemed awfully odd. But it didn't. Somehow, he had acquired a partner.

It wasn't long before the shuttle passed over again. Two wooden crates dropped out and broke apart as they bounced over the ground. The shuttle made another pass, lower this time. It chased off some birds that had come low to avoid it, and Marnie tumbled out. She rolled to a stop eight feet away and got up. "Into a group," she called out, pointing to the ground in front of her. "Move!"

John's group formed up, and was told to shut up. "My name is Marnie durNow," she said.

That caught everyone's attention. The durNow clan was part of the legend surrounding Admiral Simon Barrow, founder of the Duelists. An old woman by the name of Alicia durNow was credited with inspiring Simon Barrow, who had been condemned and was headed for prison at the age of sixteen. She'd told him something about a vision she had had for him. John didn't know the details, but he was impressed, along with the rest of the new group. DurNow was close to royalty in the Duelist trade.

"I am a Grade Five Journeyman Duelist from Bellenauer Academy," Marnie durNow said. "There will be no comments about 'Bellenaeur Belles' until you are fit to defend them, and that will probably be never. I want a clear space of five feet around each candidate." They were still in such a state of mind that many of them looked for ways to measure the distance precisely. And questions were asked. Did she mean outside edge of foot to outside edge of next foot, or elbow to elbow, assuming they all kept their arms at their sides, or nose to nose, which would create its own problems?

Marnie was patient for about twenty seconds. Then she took Red-face by the collar with one hand, moved the other hand down to his crotch, and hoisted him over her head. "Here's your yardstick!" she said. She tossed the poor fellow into the thick of the crowd. That caused some confusion, because he was certainly taller than five feet. And he refused to stay stretched out on the grass no matter how many times he was forcibly repositioned. But the think-out-louders were ignored this time. The group set some distance between them, and that turned out to be all she'd wanted to begin with.

"You, the mountain," she said next. She was pointing to John. "Step away."

When he was clear of the rest she ordered them to get out of their clothes, starting right then. "From now on you'll be wearing those." She meant the pile of white shirts and pants that had spilled out of one of the crates. "But before you get your uniforms . . . *all* of your clothes! If you're shy about your bodies you can get over that *right now*, or you can plan on running bandages and serving meals until we let you go home." Within a few seconds there were twenty-six naked bodies standing in that clearing. Glenn Charles's statistics were pretty close to the mark, as John verified with some interest at that moment. Nine of them were female. The boy and the girl who looked alike, didn't anymore. They separated to different ends of the formation.

"What about him?"

Marnie looked out over the group and sighed. "It's

not important, because . . . all right. Take your clothes off, Mountain."

John did. He wanted to know why it wasn't important for him, if it was important for the rest of them. But he didn't ask. He was stared at for a while, by people who had been wanting to know if everything was in proportion.

Marnie gave them another twenty seconds to exercise natural curiosity about one another. Then she reached into a pocket and pulled out a tiny scrap of black cloth, barely big enough to cover her palm. "This," she said, holding it over her head, "is the uniform I've worn for two death matches." That put an end to the male snickering.

"Before you get your candidate clothes," she continued, "you'll earn them." She designated John, "you-the-mountain," to gather up and pass out a bunch of foot-long wooden dowels from the second crate. The sticks were round and smooth, straight, and the number 33 was stenciled on each one. All candidates were given two of them. Marnie motioned John to stand next to her again.

"You now have a group identity," Marnie said. "Your '33' sticks are worth five points each to you. Any other stick is worth three. A second stick bearing the same number is worth nothing. When I release you—" She went quiet. Dead center over the clearing, a shuttle arrived. It hovered fifty or so feet up. Other shuttles took up stations at intervals, above the trees. They began unfurling long red banners, which hung down below them and were anchored against any wind by a thick metal bar. The banner over John's group read, *33*, in big white numerals. The sky looked like a carnival setting up. It reminded John of what Glenn Charles had told them about the future, for himself and a few others. Small gray ships hung motionless against a bright blue background, with warm yellow sunshine lighting the midway. It was a cheerful scene, and most of the group by now had a good idea of what was about to happen. The excitement level went up higher than the shuttles. John was a little depressed, though, and even more nervous about being left out.

"When I release you," Marnie said to everyone but John, "you'll go stick-hunting. The clothes cost eleven points per set. Food and water while you're here will cost you five points. A cot to sleep on will cost you another three. A blanket, another two. If you come back with no points, you're finished. Anyone caught giving away a stick is finished. Anyone not back here within ten minutes of the horns sounding again is finished. Also. There are Duelists out there watching. A few of them will be playing among you. They won't take your sticks, but they will waste your time inducing you to try for theirs. You do not have time to waste."

It must have been a timed speech, because as she spoke that last word the shuttles cut loose with the horns. The noise shook the ground and sent flocks of birds flapping up from the trees around us. Group 33 let out a combined yell and headed for the other biscuit holes.

"Brother John," Marnie said when they were all out of sight.

"Yes, ma'am?" Her face was back again to the friendly expression she'd had aboard *DOMA*.

"There are no candidate clothes big enough to fit

you. The ones you have on will have to do. You can put them back on."

"Yes, ma'am," he said, and got dressed. "I understand that. But shouldn't I be earning them with the rest of my group?"

"Earn what you already own?"

"Yes, ma'am. And food, and a cot, and a blanket." And the right to count himself in Group 33, John was thinking.

"There is no cot your size, or blanket. You must be used to that by now?"

"Of course. But I can get by. And I've always earned whatever I owned, or used. Or ate."

"As to food . . . well, we can feed you." John didn't think she'd heard anything he'd said. "But if you're really concerned." She went to the pile of remaining sticks and picked up five of them. "Twenty-one points and change," she said, holding them out.

He couldn't take them. She didn't seem surprised. "Brother John," she said, "suppose you were out with the others. How many sticks would you come back with?"

"Just enough," he said. "No more, I promise."

"All right. Now. Who out there has a reasonable chance of taking your sticks away from you?"

"No one. Not any one person, anyway. Except for the Duelists, and you said they wouldn't try."

"Suppose five of the candidates combined against you?"

"That might do it."

"I doubt it, but let's assume five is enough. Why would they do that? Two sticks can't be split five ways."

"For sport?"

She nodded her head. "I'm sure you're speaking from experience." He was. "But there's a time limit. The fact is, you'd have no one coming against you, and you'd be taking from people who have no hope of beating you. You'd feel like a fool."

"Yes, ma'am." Again, John spoke from experience.

"I could let you try to take them from me," Marnie said. "But then I'd be the fool. It would be seen as unsanctioned cruelty on my part."

There was nothing arrogant in what she said, or the way she said it. It was a simple truth they both understood.

"There must be a procedure," John said. It was a plea, more than a comment. There hadn't been a minute during the past five years that he hadn't been thinking of Landfall. Since leaving that hole of a planet he grew up on he'd worked twenty or more jobs on as many planets, moons, mining asteroids, or stations. The jobs had been to give him a base while he went after higher goals. That was to fight for prize money. After one or two fights he couldn't get bets, so he'd have to move on. He'd fought more than a hundred times, sometimes dressed in animal skins, often pelted with flying garbage and furniture, while sharps and whores sat at ringside and planned how to take the prize money away. He'd existed on free meals from well-wishers or drunks, or endured company rations, and had slept wherever he could find room to stretch out. Never private quarters, never a steady woman friend, never a decent set of clothes, or anything else that would cost money. Every bit of cash he'd earned was sitting in a special account to pay for whichever Duel School would give him a chance. He'd worked a year extra so he could afford Barrow Academy, if he was to be that lucky. Right then it looked as though it had all been a waste. His size was about to get him rejected, and exhaustion made him fall deeply into self-pity. The rest of his life stretched ahead in his mind, a long bleak road with a sharp drop-off on both sides. Down the road walked a freak, all alone. It was something he'd seen in his mind many times before. That was one of the reasons he'd wanted so badly to be a Duelist. All Duelists were freaks. Most chose to be freaks, but John didn't have a choice. The idea was that at least his road would not be empty.

"There is no 'procedure' for someone your size," Marnie said.

John couldn't answer.

Marnie knew he had something to say, though. "Well?" she pressed him.

"I was invited to test," John said bitterly. "In writing. Nobody gets to Landfall without being invited. Whatever committee *invited* me . . . they had pictures. Numbers. I'm not a surprise to you. I submitted everything they asked for."

"Really? Did you mention your hobby back on Janus, of running down horses?"

"It wasn't really a hobby, just something I had to do once in a while when they ran off."

"What about punching a bull so hard you sank your fist up to the elbow in the poor creature?"

"The bull was already dead, ma'am."

"Oh? Well, I *am* pleased to know that."

John didn't know where she'd heard those things, but he had a pretty good idea. She must have known

Herdtmacher. He felt as if everything was closing in on him. Everything that used to feel like hope inside him was somehow twisted, and had sharp edges.

"Anyway," Marnie said, "there is no procedure for *size*. That's a better way to put it. But there is one for ability. For fairness to the other candidates."

She gave him a minute to think about that.

"You're the only true giant here right now. But we've had others, in other years. All of them went out stick-hunting with everyone else. However, we have a fair idea of your strength, and your combat abilities. Testing you against other candidates would tell us nothing new about you. And it would only obscure whatever your opponent had to offer."

"So, what do I do?"

Marnie's face transformed into something colder than space. "What you're told. When you're told to do it. I've been stuck with this group and I do not intend to be embarrassed by a swollen horse turd passing itself off as a human being. Look to your life, Mountain, because leaving here alive is the best you can hope for. Clear?"

In other words, Welcome to the fold, Brother John. He grinned in relief. "Clear, ma'am."

"Oh, damn," she said. Her face reversed itself and softened again. "There's one more thing. We give out no information on a candidate until after the selection process is completed and the candidate has departed Landfall. And observers are not permitted. Thomas Klaus Herdtmacher asked me, as a personal favor, to explain that to you." John had been right. The stories about the horses and the bull had been well known on Janus. Herdtmacher had passed them on.

"He won't be here," Marnie went on. "So don't worry about that, or don't expect anything out of it, whichever applies. Clear? Good. Now it's done. This almost squares me with the old bastard. And if you ever repeat what I just said I will beat you very slowly to death. And you have had the last civility you can expect." Cold again, hard and distant like an orbiting weapons complex, but still beautiful, Marnie turned away.

Their conversation had taken only a few minutes, which was all the time Ben Slate had needed to gather his wood. He came trotting into the clearing with three sticks in each hand and that innocent-rogue grin on his face. Marnie was clearly taken by surprise. She waited for him to reach her, and examined all of the sticks. The captured ones were from Groups 41, 23, 16, and 9. In order, those were the banner numbers hanging from shuttles that formed almost a straight line out from us.

"You started with Forty-one," Marnie said to him, "and worked your way out to Nine."

"Yes, ma'am."

"And you got to each one before the candidates were fully disbursed."

"Yes, ma'am."

"Meaning you had, oh, two or three candidates to choose from near each clearing."

"Yes, ma'am. Just one, in twenty-three."

"Meaning that you fought against whoever happened to be there."

"Yes, ma'am."

"And I suppose you stopped for dinner?"

"Just some berries, ma'am."

"Back up. Three paces." When he had, she began

throwing the dowels at him two at a time, using both of her hands and launching them hard and straight. Slate caught three of them and dodged the other three.

"Toss them over there," she said. She pointed to the stack of leftover sticks. "Then pick out a set of clothes."

When he was dressed, she said, "Both of you, start running the perimeter. Stay together and don't stop until I tell you to."

John let Ben set the pace for the first circuit, then kicked it up a little. Ben grinned and stayed even, then went up a notch when they hit the starting point again. After five increases they called it even and ran side-by-side. Group 33 was straggling back into the clearing and over to Marnie, one at a time. Glenn Charles was one of the first to get back. Portly as he was, there was no jiggle to him. The little guy was solid as rock. When the horns went off, John started worrying about Linda Doya. That lasted for about a minute. She called out to him from a few feet inside the treeline and waved. She had an armful of sticks, and was strewing them around like bird feed as she trotted in the opposite direction from Ben and John. When they came around to her again after three-quarters of a circuit she ran with them until they approached Marnie and the others. She was still carrying six of the dowels.

John had always been a pretty good runner, both in distance and in speed. Ben Slate was no slouch. But Linda Doya could have been a champion at the Domain Games. As fast as John and Ben were moving by then, she had no trouble keeping up. Far from it. She ran ahead of them, backward, keeping up a chatter the whole time. "Well," she said after a while, "the time

limit's about up. Jolly times." She got in line behind
Red-face and started poking him in the back with a
stick. He ignored her.

Ben and John had established that they'd talk about
anything except their respective homes. The way
they'd both been watching Linda Doya's naked body as
she ran backward and facing them, it was pretty clear
that she was another subject they'd avoid. And they
did, for the rest of their time on Landfall.

All twenty-six who had gone out made it back before the time limit passed. The brother and sister arrived last, and together. Neither of them came back
with their own sticks, John learned later, but both had
sticks captured from other groups. That explained the
bewildered look they'd had on their faces when they
came out of the woods. They would stay in contention,
wear clothes, and eat, because of Linda's anonymous
gifts. Some hadn't been so lucky. Eight came back with
nothing. Marnie durNow lined them up, marched them
into the woods, and came back alone. They were never
seen again.

More crates fell out of the hovering shuttle before it
drew in the banner and disappeared over the treeline.
Marnie signaled for Ben and John to stop running and
join the others. It turned out that if a candidate didn't
have at least eleven points, he or she stayed naked, and
could not buy food and water or a cot. Ten points or
less bought only a blanket. That accounted for six of
the nineteen left in Group 33. The two John knew from
this group were Mark Tannen and Red-face, whose
name was Oliver Leverant. Two men and two women
made up the other four. They were assigned to gather
up the group's old clothes, including what belonged to

the eight who were gone, and stuff them in a large
canvas sack from one of the crates. Roy Billsworth was
able to buy candidate clothes and a blanket, but no food
or water. The rest, twelve in all, had deluxe accommodations. The cot was useless to John, but he wasn't allowed to give it away.

Food and water were uncrated and dispensed by the
blanket-squad of six, and Billsworth. The more successful candidates avoided their eyes as a full canteen
and a wrapped package of food were handed out. The
food consisted of a large hunk of pressed loaf that was
brown with green flecks in it. It was tastier than some
of the company rations John had lived on for months at
a time, and went down easy with the water. They were
allowed to sit on the grass and eat. The sun was just set-
tling down on the top of the treeline by then, and there
was a thin haze of cloud that looked like it was catching fire in every color there was. The day had never
been uncomfortably hot, but the evening coolness was
refreshing.

Marnie sat off by herself on her cot and read through
some papers until the light grew too dim. Then she
stripped off her Duelist uniform and stretched out on
the cot. They could hear her snoring within five minutes.

The rest took her cue. Those who had cots, and
could use them, arranged them in a large circle so their
heads would point inward to a common center. John
spread out his blanket and joined the circle. Linda took
it on herself to call the dinner servers over. It was
nearly full dark before they were all arranged. Those
who had clothes took them off again when someone

said that they would be uncomfortable the next morning if they didn't.

There was a lot of talk and laughter. John explained his special situation when asked about it, without mentioning anything about Herdtmacher. No one voiced any resentment except for Roy Billsworth. It had already been established that Group 33 didn't listen to Roy Billsworth, without a word being spoken on the subject. But still, not much conversation came his way. In a matter of hours the others had established a bond John didn't share. Tomorrow they'd be fighting one another for the honor of being selected by a real Duel School. But that didn't make any real difference in the way they laughed and joked with each other. All of them had made it through a full day at Landfall. Besides, real Duelists made friends among their own kind, didn't they?

"I'll pay for dinner, old chum," Linda called out when things had gotten giggly. "By the way, our agents have come to terms and I'll be killing you tomorrow night. Wine?"

It was Glenn Charles who answered. "Yes, a nice red, I think. And how is that gorgeous new God-child of mine? Poor thing, an orphan so soon."

Nothing was said about any of the eight who'd been rejected. John listened to Group 33 drop into sleep, one by one, and watched the stars come out the same way.

It hadn't rained, but the grass was soaked the next morning. The good news was that those who hadn't been able to buy water found plenty of leaf-puddles to lick dry. The bad news was that those who'd slept without cots were as drenched as their blankets. Billsworth and John had dry clothes to put on. Six others remained wet and would have been shivering if Marnie hadn't ordered them not to.

The brother and sister were named William and Rennie Pfit. They ran by themselves during breakfast, which was the same pressed loaf eaten during five laps of the clearing's perimeter.

"They'll be quitting this morning," Linda Doya said. "That's if Rennie agrees to."

"Why?" Ben Slate asked. If she'd just said that in ten seconds every human being in the Great Domain would be dropping dead, he couldn't have looked more skeptical and startled.

Linda, Ben, and John were running abreast at the head of the pack, with Linda in the middle. She was taking one and a half strides to Ben's one, and he was taking one and a half to every one of John's. It was a hot day already, and the sun had only been up for about an hour. There was a white mist floating up from the grass that was burned away before it reached knee-level. John couldn't remember ever hearing so many birds singing at once, loud enough to make conversation a matter of shouting. Not one of them was in sight, though. There were unidentifiable animals in the woods keeping pace with them. Every now and then John saw a flash of brown and white followed by another, about chest-high between clumps of trees. They reminded him of his one trip to Earth, when he'd been hired to provide entertainment on a sportsman's cruise. He'd watched dolphins arching from the water just beyond the ship's bow, riding the wake it made and leaving him hypnotized for most of that day. It was the most beautiful thing he'd ever seen involving living creatures.

"If I'm right," Linda told Ben, "I'll tell you why. Otherwise I'd just be embarrassing him."

"That's far beyond the realm of my thinking," Ben said. "Most people probably have fantasies about being a Duelist, but not many would want to make it their everyday, waking reality. And those who do . . . well, the fact is that most never could, even if they spent their entire youth training for it. But those of us who want to, and can . . . no one gets to Landfall who isn't pretty far advanced in both categories. So what could possibly, in a million years, in a million *universes* of possibility . . . how would anyone *want* to quit?"

"I'll tell you if I can," Linda answered.

"It's got to be something," Ben went on, "that's closer to your way of thinking than it is to mine. So I suppose if I knew you better, I could make a better guess."

"You're wasting your time, Slate," John said. He was as curious as Ron was, but he couldn't help thinking that Ben had just invited Linda Doya to bed with him. That seemed out of line.

"No one's wasting anything," Linda said. "The three of us are just talking to pass the time."

"I haven't been talking," John told her.

"That doesn't mean anything," she said.

They were just three laps into the run right then. John took off at his best speed and caught them again with half a circuit to go. By then he'd convinced himself that he had misunderstood the whole exchange. And sounded like a sulking baby. "Sorry," he said.

"You're running an extra lap," Ben pointed out.

"He needs to stretch," Linda said. "So would I, if I had his legs."

Petite little Linda Doya perched on top of Brother John's legs. The image got all three to laughing, trying to get that awful picture out of their minds, and naturally, coming up with even worse variations. Everyone passed them except for the Pfits.

"Testing time, children," Marnie announced. "We're going for a nice walk. Everyone stay close." She had them form up in a single line like baby ducks, a hand on the shoulder of the person ahead. A few yards into the woods she stopped everyone. "Let's all say our good-byes now," she said. "At least four of you won't be coming back." There were lowered eyes and mutterings for a minute or so, and then they were off again. They ended up in a clearing ten times the size of the one they knew. Thirty or so groups were already there, with more coming out of the woods. Most seemed to have fifty to seventy candidates; Marnie's was by far the smallest. Marnie showed them where to stand and walked to the center of the huge circle made by all the waiting groups. John counted sixty-one Duelists before he realized he was counting the same ones twice. They were milling around, passing papers back and forth, pointing out various candidates and laughing with each other.

Marnie's group was combined with three others. A few candidates exchanged group numbers and names. They were with 34, 51, and 9. Linda nudged John and pointed. There was Lobo Sparinada. He was naked and glaring hate-daggers at Ben Slate.

Each cluster of four groups, fifteen clusters in all, was separated from the others by about thirty feet to each side. They were all facing the center of that circle and the Duelists who stood there. Six of them, including Marnie, approached. There were no explanations or rules given.

"Ben Slate," Marnie called, "step out."

Ben walked halfway to the six Duelists and stopped. A Duelist who was about Ben's size walked out of the pack and introduced himself in a polite tone. He was Val Pediggio, Grade Six Journeyman from Lochmann Academy. He had a whispery voice that carried surprisingly well across the clearing. Every nerve and muscle in John's body was urging, "Run, fool!" But this is what they'd all come for. Or rather, come to get past.

"Don't get hurt, Val," one of Pediggio's pack-mates called out. "We need a good pot-scrubber at Kin'Te."

Most of the other comments were profane, having to do with parts of Ben Slate that Val Pediggio should rip out, or off.

"Just try to stay alive," Val said to Ben. "Are you ready?"

"Yes, sir," Ben Slate said. He took a step backward and went into a half-crouch, arms out and ready.

Val walked around him like a customer at a statuary shop. "You look strong," he said. "Very solid stance."

"Turn, Ben!" Holly Bittran called out. She was one of the two females who couldn't afford clothes. Cheryl Mansinger was the other. Neither of them seemed self-conscious anymore. "Face him. What's wrong with you?"

"He knows what he's doing," Linda told her. "Just watch his hands."

John did, and saw what she was talking about. With

every step the Duelist took, Ben's hands moved a little. Not his wrists, just his hands. It reminded John of a sundial, the way those hands followed Val Pediggio around. They marked every advance, and every time he took a step or two backward, Ben's hands went back to the position they'd been in when Val had been at that spot before.

"Why is he doing that?" Holly asked.

"He's a genius," Linda said. "Geniuses don't have reasons. They have genius."

John made a snorting sound and waited for Ben Slate to get broken.

Pediggio had made one and a half circuits around Ben when he struck. He dropped and drove his right elbow into the backs of Ben's knees. Ben was caught by surprise, there was no doubting that. But he did a strange thing. As his legs folded under him he whipped his torso around and drove his own right elbow right between Pediggio's shoulder blades. But he couldn't stop his fall, and ended up facedown in the grass.

Pediggio didn't follow through with the attack everyone expected. "All right, Slate," he said. "Let's say our positions are reversed. What would you do?"

"Death match, sir, or exhibition?"

That brought a howl of laughter from the Duelist pack. "If this had been a death match," Pediggio said, "you'd be dead and I'd be home, halfway through my dinner. If it were an exhibition match you'd be half-conscious and wondering how you lost so quick. But let's say it's an exhibition. What would you do?"

"Grapple, sir. Go for a submission hold."

"Do you know any?"

"A few, sir."

"Stand up."

Ben got up and Pediggio lay down. "All right," he said, rolling onto his stomach. "Go ahead."

Ben approached him, ready to jump back at any moment. "First, sir," he said, "I'd—"

"Words can never hurt me, Slate. Take your hold. Give me the best you've got."

It took about a second, if that. Ben launched himself the last three feet and dropped all his weight on Pediggio's back. His right arm circled under the Duelist's neck, the hand of that arm found a resting place in the crook of his left arm, and his left hand closed over the back of Pediggio's neck. He stretched his legs out between Pediggio's and pushed them outward, then snaked his calves up under the Duelist's and locked ankles with him. It was a classic position that took away any leverage from the man on the bottom. Then he pulled back and up, jerking hard to his right. John closed his eyes. The damn fool was going to break the Duelist's neck and get himself beaten to death by the others.

"Have you got it?" asked that whispery voice.

"Yes, sir," Ben said.

And then, John saw one of the most amazing exhibitions of his life. Steady and slow, but very smoothly, Pediggio got up on his knees, and stood up. Every candidate there suddenly felt pressure in his bowels. All of them knew it was not possible to get up on your knees with your legs locked out that far, especially with a man of equal weight on your back. The Duelist hadn't even used his hands to get up. Ben Slate wrapped his legs around the Duelist's waist and pulled his arms back even harder.

Pediggio walked to his compatriots, with Ben hanging on him like a cub clinging to its mother. "Look at this grip," he said. "Isn't it great?"

The five Duelists crowded in to get a closer look. "Take a look at his thumbs," a woman said. "Dug in like that. That must hurt like hell, Val."

"It does," Pediggio said. "It's excruciating. He's got the nerve, and the vein too." He could have been discussing the weather on a planet half the galaxy away. "I can't feel my legs at all."

"Really? Not much power, it looks to me."

"He's weak as an infant," Pediggio said. "But he's got bony thumbs and a good"—Ben must have tightened a notch on him just then, because he shivered a little bit—"sense of placement," he finished.

"Where'd you learn that . . . what's your name again?"

"Benjamin Slate, ma'am."

"Where'd you learn that? The thumb placement, I mean."

"I made it up, ma'am."

"Anatomical charts?" another Duelist asked.

"Yes, sir."

"Interesting."

"You're not easing off, are you?" another asked.

"No, sir. Not until Duelist Pediggio tells me to."

That brought more laughter, but there was no sneering in it this time. "Listen," Marnie said. "There are three ways your opponent can react to the way you've got Val tied up. Cede the match, go unconscious and lose that way, or break the hold. But never, *never*, *never*, do you let go because your opponent says to."

"I'm not an opponent," Pediggio said. "I'm a recruiter." His voice was weakening to the point that it was no longer easy to hear what he'd said.

"That brings up an interesting distinction, doesn't it?" Marnie asked. "On the one hand we have our oaths and our traditions, which date back to Admiral Simon Barrow. But of course he may not have foreseen a situation in which . . ." The longer she spoke, the louder came the snickering from her fellow Duelists.

Val Pediggio was weaving from side to side and front to rear. "It's time for another candidate," he said. "In the interest of time." Now he was barely audible.

After making him repeat himself five or six times, one of them said, "Go ahead, Val. We've seen it." They gave a short round of applause. For Pediggio or for Ben, no one could tell.

One of Pediggio's hands gripped Ben's right arm just below the pit. His other hand went to Ben's left leg, just up from the knee, and both hands moved like spiders crawling. All of a sudden Ben's arms and legs flailed outward like a spastic marionette. He screamed and hit the ground hard. Pediggio took a leisurely walk behind him and did something with his hands over Ben's face, then jabbed him in the lower back with his left thumb. Ben jerked up straight as a board, was yanked straight up off his feet, and Pediggio held on to his shoulders until his airborne body tilted at a 45-degree angle. Then he let go. Poor Ben hit the ground on his heels and fell backward, full-out. He landed hard and didn't move. Pediggio walked back into the pack of Duelists without a glance at Ben. None of the others looked at him, either. Marnie made a note on a piece of paper.

John tried to imagine some code or other that civilians might think was cruel, but which Duelists had thought through and understood more clearly. And he wanted to think like a Duelist. Or that the candidates were an inferior species in the hands of capricious gods. And he wanted to think like a god. For something like those reasons, he didn't even consider going to help Ben Slate. No candidate went, except for Linda Doya. John was occupied with looking into the Duelist pack and wondering which face belonged to his personal tormentor.

But then Linda called for him to help. Ben had gone into spasms and was vomiting through his mouth and nose. John lifted him by the back of his pants and held him facedown off the ground so he could empty himself without choking. After a while Ben took in a long breath and said he was okay. When John set him down he jumped to his feet. He stripped off his soaked shirt and threw it toward the Duelists. A few of them looked over at him and grinned, then ignored him. He stood there for a minute with his fists balled up at his sides, and came back to stand with his friends.

Lobo Sparinada's laughter sounded like a stuck wheel being wrenched free. When Roy Billsworth started cackling, Mark Tannen slapped him in the back of the head and dared him to do anything about it. He didn't.

Linda gave John another one of her looks, and her expression helped him to figure out what he was feeling: Helplessness and shame, fear and moral paralysis. He hadn't gone to Ben Slate before Linda called for his help. He had feared rejection for breaking ranks. And Slate hadn't even said thank you.

"Brother John. Step out."

He was back in Dennis Town, stepping into the combat circle to face Thomas Klaus Herdtmacher. The heat of the day was almost the same, but this time it was full daylight. Then he'd been fighting for all the people he called family. This time it was just for himself. This time no one's life depended on what he was about to do except his own. That should have made it easier, but it didn't. He'd had five years to think about this moment and had pictured it in a thousand different ways. Losing, winning, apologizing to the spouse and children of the Duelist he'd crippled, lying in a hospital and learning from Dr. Samuels he'd never walk again or have children of his own, Herdtmacher deeply ashamed of him in either case, laughing because it had been so easy, slinking off somewhere to commit suicide, Sister Kim the one constant, always there and offering advice he could never hear.

Dimly, John was aware of other tests going on in the field at that moment. He took a deep breath and found himself standing where Slate had been just a few minutes before.

"Just try to stay alive. Are you ready?"

John was sure the Duelist had introduced himself but he couldn't remember. The man was big, as normal people go. Six foot three or so, probably two hundred fifty pounds. He hadn't been in the Duelist pack that was working with Marnie's group, John would have remembered that thick black beard and bald scalp. And the scar that crossed his bare chest from left shoulder to right waist, and looked like a dry red riverbed seen from orbit. I've fought bigger and worse, was what John thought. And he laughed, on the verge of tears. He had never pictured himself having a last thought that was quite that stupid.

"Yes, sir," he said.

John's mouth was still open from answering when the Duelist hit him the first time. The second and third blow to the mouth again, and the fourth and fifth to the chest, all landed before he felt the first one. John thought it was very kind of his adversary to sit down and give him time to spit out a tooth and a mouthful of blood. The Duelist pack thought it was hilarious.

John was spitting a second time when he noticed the blood on the left side of the Duelist's face. It was flowing from a nasty little gash that looked like a red river on a white desert. He was sitting with his hands up on his knees and smiling. The knuckles of John's right fist were a little sore. Not bad, he thought.

The Duelist got up again and walked backward toward John. "See it coming," he said. He was looking at his compatriots, not at John, so maybe they saw it coming. John didn't. His right heel made a cave in John's belly and sent him airborne. His arms and legs flew straight out in front of him, and his hands seemed to grope for his feet. He hit the ground and tumbled backward, just able to make a roll that put him back on his feet.

The Duelist was talking with his counterparts, and somehow John could hear every word. He couldn't believe what he was hearing. But it was confirmed when the Duelist took a step backward and collapsed. He wouldn't take any of the hands reaching down to help him. Then he looked back at John. His expression wasn't hatred, or even anger. It was the way you might look at a three-headed dog. Pity for the poor creature, wonder that it could exist. A little disgust.

The Duelist got up on his left leg and hopped off the field. A shuttle dropped down and he was loaded aboard, then it took off again. Word got around very fast that Grade Six Journeyman Duelist J. T. Derringer of Morrow Academy had kicked Brother John so hard he'd driven his thigh bone upward and shattered his hip. The other Duelists had been cursing him for being so clumsy, for demeaning the profession by getting himself hurt on a mere candidate. He had been apologizing to them. Nothing was said to John, although it dawned on him later that he should have been dead.

At that moment, standing there, John was deeply depressed. The one thing he'd wanted to do was to prove that he was more than big and strong. He'd wanted to be seen as *trainable*. But all he'd proved was that he could hit back and was hard to knock down. He needed another chance. "Can I have another Duelist?" he begged Marnie. *"Please?"*

Blank faces, then the howling laughter started with her. It spread to her comrades and then to the cluster of groups, then as quick as fire across the whole clearing as the story spread. Every head was turned in John's direction. He would have stomped off the field, bound for suicide, if Linda hadn't leaped up onto his back. "They're laughing *with* you, Brother John," she whispered in his ear. *"With* you. Your reputation is *made*. Laugh *back*, fool. *Do* something they'll remember."

John still didn't understand, but he trusted Linda Doya. He threw back his head and roared at the whole field of candidates and every Duelist there. He pawed the air and scraped the ground like a wounded mountaintooth, as he had before the fight with Herdtmacher. Louder and louder it got, until the birds shook out of the trees again and scolded everyone for ruining their morning.

John didn't know then how to end what would become his trademark. So he kept it up until Linda pounded his sides with her heels and screamed that it was enough.

When the noise settled down again the Duelists began reading from their lists. "Glenn Charles, here," pointing to a spot on the grass. "Rechaud Marrieme, here." They'd take a few steps and set up the next bout, calling out names from the cluster of groups. "Holly Bittran, here. Wayne Brzevsky, here." And so on, until about a third of the candidates were facing opponents. The same thing was going on all across the field. "Commence!" Again, no rules, no explanations.

A wave of dizziness and nausea swept over John and he found himself sitting on the grass at the front of the cluster. Marnie and one or two of her comrades glanced his way a few times but didn't order him to stand again. He kept waving and grinning at them because he was scared to death they'd call a medico and have him taken away.

The first three rounds gave just about everyone a chance to fight. This was single-elimination. The losers were ordered to turn in their candidate clothes, if they had any, and go stand by themselves in a tight-packed clump of bodies that grew every time a Duelist shouted, "Stop!" Simple bleeding was ignored, but about a fifth of the losers were either unconscious or couldn't walk. They were stripped and dragged by their fellows into the clump. Eventually a shuttle landed and they were carried aboard. Then two shuttles, then three, up to eight. Then the eight left the ground and returned again for more as the day wore on.

John drifted in and out of consciousness for most of that day. One second he'd think he was running in a billow of dust with Sister Kim, and the next he'd be jerked back to the present by the crying and shrieking as losers were declared. The game changed now, to double-elimination. Two losses and you were gone. John was left with a jumble of impressions that have never fit themselves into a whole picture: Glenn Charles down on one knee, taking blows to the head, then lashing out and freezing in what looked like a pose, a candidate impaled on his thick arm. Roy Billsworth squatting on a man's chest, beating his face with both fists until he was yanked off long after the man was unconscious. Cheryl Mansinger and Holly Bittran using a lot of bouncing moves against male opponents, using their natural assets to distract them. Then moving in and winning. William and Rennie Pfit. Both reluctant but devils when hit. Red-faced Oliver Leverant on his back, coordinating his right instep with a standing opponent's nose to produce what looked like a squashed tomato. Linda Doya elegant and always in the air, always. The only candidate with no grass-stains.

And Mark Tannen, taking a fist to the throat. Nodding to Linda and a few others that he was all right. Waving away help. Turning away and walking toward the medical shuttle, collapsing and dead before he reached it.

Ben Slate was called out once again just before the sun reached the treeline. The fighting field was empty

of candidates by then. Those who had survived the day
sprawled out or stretched out on the grass. They were
William and Rennie Pfit, Roy Billsworth, Cheryl
Mansinger, Glenn Charles, Oliver Leverant, Linda
Doya, and Ben Slate and John. The others were somewhere in a four-abreast line of naked people that
snaked back and forth across the far side of the clearing. All but Mark Tannen. At the head of the snake,
shuttles loaded, took off, and the snake became a little
smaller. It reminded John of a scary book Sister Kim
used to read. *Dante's Inferno*, he thought he remembered being its name.

Ben's opponent looked as rested as he was. He trotted over from about a quarter of the way around the
clearing with a big smile on his face. "Hello, everyone," he said. "My name is Peter McMillan." By then
Group 33 had shrunk, or grown, depending on how you
looked at it, to Team 33. They gave McMillan blank
stares and silence. McMillan was a good-sized kid with
skin as dark as Linda's and a voice as strong as red-
faced Oliver's. Marnie and a Journeyman Duelist
named George Canby from Lochmann Academy were
to judge the combat. This time, there were rules.

"You'll fight for two-minute intervals," Canby told
them. "Then you'll run to that red pole"—which was
about six hundred yards away—"pull a string from it,
and return here. The process will be repeated until one
of you is unable to continue. Questions?"

McMillan opened his mouth to speak and Canby
told him if he lost, he had better not return to his group.
Marnie told Ben the same thing. Canby shouted, "Commence!"

From the beginning it was clear that the two were

evenly matched. Both were as quick as thought with their hands, powerful with their feet, and neither one was the slightest bit shy or hesitant. It seemed only a few seconds had passed when Marnie called out, "Run!"

It took Ben two hundred nineteen seconds to get back, with McMillan twenty-two seconds behind. He never stopped running, but tossed a piece of red string on the grass and jumped with both feet aimed at Ben's chest. Slate rolled under him and jumped to his feet, and they squared again. Neither one of them was able to land a clear-cut blow. John was in awe of how fast they could throw, recover, dodge, strike out, follow through, recover, turn, block, dodge. . . . "Run!" McMillan's group got up and congregated near everyone, leaving about thirty feet between the group and them.

After the fifteenth circuit it was getting dark and we were the only people left at the clearing. Marnie announced that she was bored. Canby agreed with her. They gave the combatants five seconds to rest and explained to them that they were to continue, alone and on their honor, until the match was decided. Then, "Run!" Canby waved his arm at the woods behind. Lights came on from the trees and illuminated that half of the clearing.

"Let's go, children," Marnie said. They clanked and popped and groaned to their feet and Group 33, except for Ben, quit the field for the day.

Bloodied but unbowed, humble but not humbled. Isn't that the saying? Anyway, Marnie's team went home.

"Here he is," Linda Doya said an hour later. John

was stretched over two cots set end to end, beneath two blankets that overlapped in the middle. The extras were gifts from Marnie. His bunched-up clothes made a nice pillow.

"I want you to listen and tell us what you think," Linda said to John. Richard Pfit was right behind her. "Go on, Richard," she said.

"I explained it to Rennie," he began. "She can't make up her mind. Linda said I could talk to you."

Linda said I could talk to you. Not "should," which would be strange enough. But "could." An audience had been requested, and Linda Doya had granted it. If John had sat up and found something like a scepter to hold, Richard might have nodded and touched a knee to the ground. John fought a powerful urge to giggle.

"Go ahead," John said to Richard, feeling foolish. But then, Linda had come to him with this deep secret, and not to Benjamin Ronald Slate. That was worth a lot.

"It was the stick-hunt," Richard said. "I guess you know I lost everything."

John also knew that Rennie had lost everything, but he didn't mention it. Everyone knew what had happened, including Marnie, but there hadn't been a word spoken about it. Even Roy Billsworth had found something to like about the Pfits. Linda had gathered extra sticks for them by convincing candidates returning to their groups to give her the ones they couldn't spend, and weren't permitted to give away. It could be said that she hadn't "won" them, but no one was saying it.

"I lost both of my Thirty-threes," Richard said. "All I had was a three-pointer I'd taken from a kid who had a handful of them. Then someone came after that one stick I had. I'm not sure I can explain this, Brother John. But that stick is *all* I had. I was naked and hungry. Losing that one stick meant I'd have to go home beaten and humiliated. See what I mean? It was all I had in the world. Everything I *had*. And this kid wanted it. Not because he needed it. Just wanted it. Wanted to take it *from* me."

"I understand," John said. Richard had been angry enough to kill, and that had frightened him.

"Linda said you would. I was so . . . so *sick*. You knew what it would be like. That's the real reason they didn't send you out. You already knew. But the rest of us . . . It wasn't until then that I understood why they set it up the way they did. To make us take *everything* from somebody. That's the same as killing. And that kid's eyes, when we squared off. He knew he could do it. He didn't need to. But he knew he could. That's why he did it. Ever since then . . . I think about that kid's eyes, the way he was looking at me. If I become a Duelist . . . my eyes have to get like that, don't they? I have to be able to do what he did to me. Look at somebody, and take everything they have. And everything they want, everything they ever dreamed about, and everything their families are expecting them to be . . . not because I *need* to. Just because I *can*."

John wanted no part of this, now or ever again. "What do you want?" he asked harshly. A mountaintooth again, with a dry throat. No one expected a mountaintooth to have a conscience. It helped.

Richard jumped back as if he'd been struck. "I was hoping . . . ah, I see. It's my question, my answer. What

Rennie does is up to her." He turned around, but then Linda gave John another one of her looks. She was about to start another tour of the Inferno when Richard started talking again. "See, Rennie and I grew up as wards of the government. That was in this, I guess you'd say bureaucratic hive, that called itself a home. That was in a little pseudo-town the good citizens of Beecham paid to have dug into a stretch of useless tundra. We had each other and a book about Duelists and another one about acrobats. We used to practice. A *lot*. Sending us here could get recognition and maybe more money for the . . . the hive. On the day we left, we finally saw it from the air. It looked like an acne sore. I don't want to go back. Rennie doesn't either. But we have to, until we're twenty. I mean, we have to if we quit or we don't make it. It looks like we'll make it. If we don't quit."

"Richard," John said to his back. "None of us has made it yet. And Duelist training is five years. You'd be past twenty. I don't think the academies make you kill anyone. Not on purpose, anyway."

He started walking again and didn't look back.

"Please don't do that anymore," John begged Linda.

"Why not? You did all right. With practice you could be good at it."

"I don't want to be good at it," he said. "That is the last thing in the Great Domain I ever want to be good at. Let me say it again. This time without the 'please.' Don't do that anymore."

"All right, Brother John." She wasn't angry, but seemed disappointed. "From now on when people want to talk to you, I'll just say—"

"They won't." John turned away on his side. He fell

asleep thinking about seeds, and ideas. And what they could grow into if you weren't careful.

John woke up with the first light. He had swung his legs over the side of the cot and meant to stand up when a thought the size of a planet dropped on him. It had been hovering out there all night, growing in the darkness.

He didn't have to look to know that Linda was gone. He found her sitting in the woods, balled up with her elbows on her knees and her face hung down between them. John picked her up and cradled her in his arms like an infant. There wasn't anything to say that would be enough. She had offered him the greatest gift she could bestow on another human being—a gift more intimate than the secrets of her body. She had offered him a share in what she *was*, and in allowing him to be this close she helped him to understand what it meant to become truly Brother John.

"I couldn't sleep," she said, resting her head against his chest.

"I know," he said. "Linda, I am so . . ."

"I . . . I thought he'd be back. Who could beat Ben Slate? But he never came back. And I don't know how to get to that clearing where . . . Hey! Why did you drop me? What's wrong with you? That was nice."

Thoughts as weighty as planets? That grow in the darkness? Damned *balloons!* I am Brother John, and thank you very much. Ashamed to show how much it mattered to him that Linda was thinking only of Ben Slate, John got to work.

He drank half of a full canteen of water and

watched Roy and Cheryl and Oliver licking the grass before they did their five laps. Then there was breakfast again, the last on Landfall. Marnie led the eight of them back through the woods. Their final test, whatever that was to be, was just ahead. John pushed Linda Doya out of his thoughts. The singing started with eight different songs and they finally compromised on one that most of them knew. Marnie sang along. She stopped them when the clearing was in sight but still thirty feet away. "Billsworth!"

Roy took a couple of steps out of the duckling line.

"Open your mouth," Marnie ordered. Maybe he was too slow. She clamped a hand under his jaw and his mouth flew open like a beached fish. Then she pushed him double over and jammed a finger up his throat. He gagged a few times, and vomited.

"Pick it up," Marnie said. "Just the chunks."

Whatever he was about to say was choked off by her hand at the back of his neck. He yelped and did as commanded.

"What is that?" Marnie asked him in a sweet voice.

"Tree bark, ma'am. I was *youch!*"

"Tree bark," Marnie said. "Is this tree bark formulated by the finest nutritional minds in the Great Domain, expertly pressed into logs, and then lovingly boiled in vats the size of shuttles? Is that the tree bark this is, Billsworth?"

"Yes, ma'am."

"Good. Now I understand. Eat it again."

He did, and started gagging again.

"You are rejected," Marnie said. "Leave your candidate clothes here. Then you're free to go where you choose."

Roy Billsworth turned flaming red. He swung his right fist at her and found himself lifted by that elbow and the crotch of his pants, and held over Marnie's head. She only tossed him about six feet. He landed on his back, got up on his hands and feet, and backed away. "The clothes," she said in that same sweet tone. "Five . . . four . . ."

He beat the deadline by less than a second. After that he was gone, running parallel to the clearing. "Whoever dropped that food," Marnie said as we formed the line again, "didn't do Billsworth any favors. But on behalf of my noble profession, thank you." That was another joke, John was beginning to learn, like the ones about "brief rides" and "comfort" she'd used to begin their acquaintance. A group proctor could reject a candidate in her charge at any time, for any reason or for no reason, but the illicit food gave Marnie excellent grounds to get rid of the troublemaker Billsworth.

The group was about to be given a couple of surprises.

The first was pointed out, "Hey, *look!*" by Glenn Charles. About three-quarters of the way between the distant red pole and Group 33, Peter McMillan was making his way toward the group. He looked horrible, stumbling and straining like a dying man. His legs wouldn't straighten and he was hunched over and wobbling from side to side. Every few feet he steadied himself by putting his hands on the ground and pausing. About ten yards behind him was Ben Slate, who looked just as bad. The red pole wasn't red anymore, though. It was stripped to white. The grass where they'd been sitting the night before was scattered with foot-long lengths of red string.

McMillan's group hadn't arrived yet. Group 33 began yelling encouragement to Ben. As the two men got closer, everyone could see the blood spattered on their faces and arms. Both had thrown their shirts away. Ben saw his group, or heard them, and gave a half wave before his arm fell down by his side and swung limply like the other one.

After a few seconds they stopped calling out. Glenn Charles explained why. "Neither of them can lose this fight now," he said. He was right. It felt indecent to root against Peter, even for the sake of Ben.

"Unless," Doya said.

"Exactly," Charles said, shooting her a smile. "Exactly."

"Unless" is what happened right then.

Benjamin Ronald Slate ended that fight in a way that was to live in Duelist chatter as long as Brother John's mountaintooth performance. Still running like a dying man, his body began to straighten. From his right-side pocket he withdrew a thick red cord about six feet long. Peter gave no indication that he heard Ben coming up from behind him. Ben tackled him, and they rolled together for ten feet or more. Then Ben got to his feet. Peter tried. He got halfway up and Ben yanked on the rope. Peter's ankles were tied together. He fell like dead weight. Ben closed in. Peter got up on his knees and raised his arms protectively over his head. Ben circled behind him and stayed behind him, moving to either side every time Peter tried to turn and face him. Peter tried to stand. Ben jerked on the rope. Peter's legs flew out from under him. Again, and again. Peter wouldn't quit. But Peter was finished.

And Ben wouldn't attack. He looked toward Marnie

and held up his arms in supplication. "Draw!" he cried
out. "Declare a draw!"

George Canby came running out of the woods just
opposite where Ben and Peter were. "No draw!" he
called out. He took Ben by the arms and half dragged
him over to Group 33. "You've got the winner," he told
Marnie. "But by God, I've got a student for Lochmann
Academy!" He gave Ben's shoulders a squeeze and ran
back to Peter McMillan. By then Peter had untied himself and was standing, still wobbling. He held up the
rope and pointed to it with his other hand. He called out
in a voice that barely reached us. "Sneaky bastard! You
should have told me you can knit!"

"It's called splicing, you bonehead!" Slate called
back. "Why do you think I let you run ahead of me all
night? You think you're faster than me? You couldn't
outrun a—" His wheezing kept him from finishing, and
he collapsed, laughing.

"I'll get you!" he said, curling into a ball and pounding the ground. "I'll get you!"

Canby led Peter to his group, which was just coming
out of the woods. They circled around him and lifted
him up on two candidates' shoulders. Peter was smiling. He looked like he belonged where he was, and he
looked like he knew it.

But Group 33 had a bigger hero, and bigger shoulders. Linda Doya kicked at John's legs and pointed
until John understood that she wanted him down on the
ground on all fours. They loaded a grinning Ben Slate
up onto John's shoulders, John stood back up, and
Group 33 took the field.

From around the perimeter other groups were filing
into place. They were a much smaller crowd than the

morning before. Only one morning before? It seemed
like months ago. But there were still too many candidates there for the number of school slots available.
The Duelists had promised an eighty percent reduction,
which would bring the number of candidates down to
ninety-six hundred. Twelve schools, eight hundred
each. No more. Glenn Charles estimated that there
were still about fifteen thousand candidates, by the
time the groups had all arrived.

The murmuring that had been going on rose to
shouts: profane, insulting, good-natured, personal, gen-
eral, and all of them serious. The candidates wanted to
get this thing done. Group 33 was still the smallest, and
working on being the loudest. In a burst of team spirit
they voted Peter McMillan one of them. Now they
were invincible. If war was to come, then let it come,
fast, hard, and unmerciful. The morning was bright and
hot with a stiff breeze blowing in from the east. It
seemed right for a war.

The birds set up a clamor of their own but this time
they refused to be relocated. They had their territory.
So did the teams.

The second surprise had to do with the way the field
was set up. Now that Group 33 was complete and
strong and in spirit, with Ben Slate safely back again
and their challenges still echoing over the grass, they
gave this second surprise some attention. At the center
of the clearing were three shuttles parked in a triangle
so that each bow touched the stern of the next one. A
flagpole of about fifty feet stood up from the center of
the shuttles. There were chairs everywhere. About
thirty of them were gold, set off by themselves to the
right of the shuttles. Twice that number of chairs, were

white and made up another block set off by themselves.
And then there were the gray ones—thousands of gray
chairs facing outward from the shuttles, set up in neat
ranks and files with plenty of walking room between
them.

Marnie durNow left the group and headed for the
shuttles. She was about halfway there when dozens of
shuttles began flying over in triangular formations.
Those horns sounded again. Marnie and other Duelists
who'd left their groups froze in place. A little speck
crawled up the flagpole and fell open into a flag that
must have been twenty feet high and thirty long. The
wind snapped at it a few times, and caught. It was the
Duelist flag, the first real one John had ever seen. A
broad white field held blue semicircles like parentheses
out toward either side. In between, a black sword stood
on its haft, and tilted inward at a 45-degree angle. A
black pike stood at an angle just opposite, point-up and
crossing the sword at the center of the flag.

The horns quit, all at once. There was a dead silence
all across the clearing except for the sound of that flag
cracking and snapping in the breeze. It was all the candidates could do to keep from cheering, but they knew
better. The Duelist Emblem was a sacred thing. It was
the family crest of the Barrow clan, the personal repre-
sentation of Admiral Simon Barrow. "Saint Barrow,"
Founder of the Duelists, first and foremost among the
living twenty-three thousand men and women who carried that title; first and foremost among the thousands
upon thousands no longer living, whose lives and
deaths made up so much of the history and the mythol-
ogy of the Great Domain. Simon Barrow, "Destiny's
Catalyst," whose band of anarchists challenged and

broke the power of Earth and thus created the Great
Domain. Simon Barrow. Whose reward was to be
stripped of everything he held dear and to be cast aside
like a viper from the garden. Until he came back, wiser
than when he'd left, more patient, kinder, more diplo-
matic, and madder than hell.

That was history. This was now. Still, the reality of
Simon Barrow himself was there on that field.

The candidates had wanted a war just minutes ago.
Now with Simon Barrow's flag there, and the thick,
warm, thrilling feeling that he himself was watching . . . now they shattered the silence and began
screaming for WAR. "Let *us*, the worthy, identify and
expel the last batch of rejects. Some standing here but
did not deserve to share the field with Simon Barrow.
Pretenders. Scum. Maggots. *Losers*. That flag is *ours!*"

The birds, obviously impressed, flew overhead and
peppered everyone again.

Marnie and the other Duelists continued their walk
toward the shuttles. They somehow seemed to be growing taller, even as their bodies were shrinking against
the backdrop of that flag. The candidates could hear a
lot of laughter and see a lot of jostling as the Duelists
formed into three-abreast lines and entered the shuttles.
There were insults shouted so loud the candidates
could hear them over their own talk, shoves so savage
they would ordinarily have led to someone's death, and
above it all more of that strange we-are-one laughter
that was so magnetic the candidates intended to kill one
another to join it. Each candidate stood a little taller
too, not that John needed that as a goal. The Duelists
came out again about ten minutes later. Each of them
was carrying two white bags, a big one and a small one.

"Listen for your name," Marnie instructed. That didn't take long, with only eight left in the group. They lined up in the order their names had been called. Marnie started with Oliver Leverant and Cheryl Mansinger, at the head of the line. The first thing they were given was a wrapped package. Clothes. Neither of them seemed especially impressed or eager to put them on. Their nudity had set them apart, and was a badge of the extra suffering they'd been undergoing. They seemed almost to have become proud of it. But they dressed when Marnie told them to. There was a clean uniform for Ben, who needed it. Then, from the larger bag, came the dumbest-looking hats anyone had ever seen. They groaned when Marnie made it perfectly clear that they were going to wear them. How could anyone have a serious war with those silly hats on their heads? They were white. Take two pancakes, a big one and a little one. Put the little one in the center of the big one and lift it up about three inches. Add a little stiff material to connect them. Then around that material, tie a blue ribbon with a forked end like a snake's tongue. Then, if you dare and you have no pride at all, put the thing on your head. Group 33 accepted the hats with suspicion and distaste on every face. They swapped them back and forth until everyone had one that fit reasonably well.

Luckily for John, none of them fit. Not even close. The biggest hat there sat on his head like a wafer and slid off every time he moved, which he made sure to do every time Marnie was looking his way. "Carry it," she said at last. "Just carry the damned thing."

"To where?" John asked.

She jerked a thumb behind her. "There."

There were other people starting to file out of the shuttles now. Most of them were dressed in formal Duelist attire—broad-shouldered tunics drawn in at the waist with thick leather belts and cinched with big buckles that bore circular Duelist emblems of polished silver and jade. Gray trousers that tucked into wide-holed black boots cut just below the knee. Brown leather wrist-guards that covered half the forearm. Wing-mantled shoulders.

Deep crimson tunics identified the wearer as a Grade Two Expert; there were a lot of those. Royal blue tunics signified a Grade One Expert; there were not so many of those. Royal blue-edged in silver meant the wearer was one step away from the ultimate rank of Master. There were two of those.

When the last of these Senior Duelists walked out into the sunshine, the others made room for him like the parting of the Dead Sea. No one got within eight feet of him. That was because by tradition, at least for show, a closer approach was seen and responded to as a direct challenge. In other words, suicide. This particular man did not "bear" a rank; he *was* the rank. The ultimate one. A Master Duelist. This particular man wasn't large. A little taller than average, short gray hair, Oriental eyes, long thick arms, thin graceful waist and legs. John was not close enough to see him in detail, but any aspiring Duelist would know Chen Shen just from the way he moved. White tunic—this time signifying purity and simplicity, the ancient principle of *maru,* the colors out and then back again, like ships, completing and fulfilling the circle. And the Master's Belt. A rainbow around his waist studded with gems. No buckle. Tied off in a one-of-a-kind knot. Hu-

mankind in its most lethal form, personified. Chen
Shen's statistics were carried and updated in books that
few people needed to refer to. He had made six-
hundred-plus registered kills in formal combat.

The others wore gold medallions around their necks.
Etched Roman numerals announced their own tally of
registered kills. DLX, CCC, and so on. Below "C"-
level, the saying was, no Duelist dared to wear a medallion for fear of drowning in ridicule.

Richard Pfit nudged John in the back and whispered,
"I changed my mind." Linda Doya kicked the back of
his leg and gave him a thumbs-up sign. From the
smaller bag Marnie durNow pulled out a stack of eight-
by-eight-inch placards strung with a length of cord.
The cords slipped over the candidates' necks. The placards carried their names in large letters. Below each
name was printed the name of candidates they'd fought
the day before, in red ink for battles won, yellow for
battles lost. John's bore his own name, and nothing
else. Ben's carried the name of Peter McMillan in red.
Linda's had four red names, one yellow one. Glenn
Charles's placard bore six names in red. And Cheryl
Mansinger, whom John had stopped paying attention
to, led all of the rest. Eight red names, no yellow ones.
John was shocked to see how much fun he'd missed
while he was flitting from one phase of insensibility to
another.

With the stupid hats, and now the placards, the obvious was starting to penetrate into the candidates'
minds. Anyone who has been in combat or has been
swept up to the brink of it will understand why it took
so much to change their thinking. Every ounce of their
adrenaline was screaming for war. Glory lay before

them in the center of that clearing. The flag snapped and *whooomphed* above them, and whispered their names. Out on the field, disgracefully still among the group, were those who needed to be eliminated before the victors could take a step closer to that glory. But now they began to understand that this was not to be. Something was horribly wrong. No war. No acts of astounding courage performed for the elite of the elite. "Who *is* that? Blessed Saint Barrow, *recruit* him!" No scum-smashing. Something was horribly, *horribly* wrong. They were *graduating*. With the unnamed scum still among them.

It wasn't much of a graduation speech, either.

"Good luck," Marnie said. Then she turned and walked away.

She had gone about ten paces, which was further than she might have expected, before the questions flew at her like angry birds riding hurricane winds. It took her a few minutes just to settle everyone down. "We proctors have done our parts," she said. "Now it's up to the individual schools. Two-thirds of you will be invited to join at least one academy. The rest . . ." She shrugged her shoulders. "But those not selected *will* have priority in applying for Landfall next year. However, I wouldn't bother if I were you. If you've come this far and no school wants you . . ." The shrug again. "There has to be a reason. It's happened, though. People have come back here and been accepted after failing previously. Nothing's impossible."

Marnie seemed to change her mind about leaving without good-byes. She came to each candidate and shook hands. "For what it's worth," she said as she passed through the line, "if it were up to me I'd take all but one of you. You don't need to know who that one is. Now. This process is going to take the rest of the daylight hours. Those gray chairs are for you. See those tables?" She pointed back toward the shuttles where a series of long tables was being set up. "In a while there'll be food and punch set out. Eat all you want. If you haven't eaten lately go slow, or you'll disgrace yourselves. The school reps will find you if they want you. Do *not* go after *them*. There will be twelve combat circles painted on the grass, one for every school. After you've committed to a school you will toss your hat inside the appropriate circle. You'll get it back when, or if, you graduate. So be sure your name is written inside. Sit wherever you want to, but not in the white chairs or the gold ones. The shuttles will begin loading after sunset, from right here, to take you up to the liners you arrived on. Your old clothes will be in a pile somewhere." Like her introductory speech aboard *DOMA*, her sentences fell together in no particular order, but she made a lot of sense in the end. Finally she said, "I do wish each of you good luck. You're fine people. Some of you I'll be seeing again, especially you females, if you're picked for Bellenauer. And for God's sake, if you're offered Bellenauer, *accept*. Don't wait for Barrow. Some of you I may have to kill one day. But the odds of that are pretty small. I intend to be a Master around the time you're graduating. I'll only be fighting against Experts then. Losers like you won't interest me then, any more than you do now." She waited a few seconds and said, "It's all right, children. That was a joke. You can laugh." They did, politely. "Good-bye, then. I'll be talking to some of you at the reception." And she left.

So that's what it was. A "reception." Linda Doya produced a pen. They all wrote their names in the hats and then stood there, looking at one another. They were free.

But no one moved. Group 33 was frozen in that moment like a completed but fragile work of art. Any movement might break it, might mean Group 33 would no longer exist. John waited for someone to start the blubbering and hugging so he could make a show of walking away in disgust. No one did that, either. Finally there was a sort of mutual shrug. Group 33 was officially done with. They headed for the waiting, the food, and the future.

You could never imagine a nicer bunch of killers.
    The candidate-pile maintaining that eight-foot-distance tradition around Chen Shen was so thick that John could barely see the man, so with his fourth plate of lobster he circulated. It was like walking through a museum gallery. Here, the woman who'd killed Myles Westover *and* Pele Pele, in the same night. Discussing that historic achievement? No. Lecturing on the relative merits of coffees produced by different worlds in the Pacifico Belt. (She owned plantations on three of those worlds.) There, three candidates combining all their weight to pull down the arm of Rene Morgenthaugh, Grade One Expert, a pinch-faced bald man no bigger than Ben Slate. The arm was immobile as stone. Everywhere, a lot of laughter and white teeth and little polite bows and "Oh *that?* It was really nothing . . . simple tricks, you'll learn them." Or, "Your uncle, eh? Well, a family tradition, then." Back to Chen Shen, the

candidate-pile smaller now. He was reciting from one of the children's historical novels he'd written. These, and not corpses-in-the-making, were his real love, it was rumored. But children's stories were not of much interest to killers-in-the-making, most of them even younger than John's grizzled nineteen years.

Incredible displays, everywhere he looked, showcased the past, present, and future of the profession.

The thirty gold chairs were filled with school administrators and their staffs. No one was approaching them except for Journeyman Duelists running in for a quick whisper and then running off again. Sheets of paper were passed around and nodded at or pointed to. These Journeymen and the people they were talking with in the chairs were the Duelists the candidates had been told not to go after. The Journeymen did the tracking down and shoulder-tapping out on the field.

John would hear a "Yes! *Yes!*!" from somewhere on the field. Candidates would go whizzing by, grinning and leaping like ecstatic gazelles. At first just a few, then more, and more, like atoms in an old-time reactor going active and colliding. Handshakes, hugs, real blubbering.

"Yes! Yes!!"

"Both schools want me!"

"It was my sister's school!"

"Yes, but I'm still hoping for Barrow."

That last was the comment John heard the most from the ecstatic gazelles. Barrow Academy, circling Teli Centauri was known as the hardest place in the universe to get to—not because of location, but because it was Barrow Academy. Tracing its roots to the person of Simon Barrow, it produced the best of the best. Even the next best school, Miyoshi, was several layers down in reputation.

John wandered back to the gray chairs after a couple of hours and took two seats next to Ben Slate. Ben was talking with Peter McMillan. Both of them looked dejected. Like Ben, Peter was wearing new clothes. His face was badly bruised and his left eye was swollen almost shut. A line of stitches made a third eyebrow above the other two. Slate looked a little better, but not much.

Ben stood up and introduced John to Peter.

"How many offers have you got so far, Brother John?" Peter asked as they shook hands.

Judging from the tone of their voices, John thought he'd picked the right company to share his anxiety. "None yet," he said. He thought to make them a little more comfortable by adding, "But the sun's still got a long way to go."

"Oh," Peter said. "Well, sure. It's not nearly over, is it? I wouldn't be worried. No, not at all."

"Not at all," Ben echoed.

Both of them snuck quick looks at John's blank placard. That's when John noticed that Ben's was gone. He was accepting no more offers. But he still wore his hat, indicating that he hadn't committed yet.

The only thing John could do was to pretend he'd known all along. "I just wanted to say congratulations," he said. "Same school?"

"We're not sure," Peter said. "We've both got offers from Lochmann, and Kin'Te. But I'm leaning to Miyoshi. If Barrow hits me too, then it will be set."

"Sure," John said. "Barrow would be the best way."

Peter's right eyebrow arched up a little in response.

It was an eerie face he made, just for a second, as if he had eaten something pretty bad and had it stick in his throat. John wondered whether Ben had hurt him more than Peter was letting on. He stopped looking up, as if it had been painful to hold his head in that position. Ben seemed to be having the same thought. He looked very concerned about his new friend. "The best way," Peter said, with that sour look. "You're telling me . . . is that what you're doing?" That's when he lowered his head. "You're telling *me* what school *I* should accept?" He'd lost track of the conversation. Ben looked worried about him.

"I agree with both of you," John told him. "You have other offers, but Barrow means no compromise. And you'll be studying together."

"Of course," Peter said. "Obviously." Now he just looked embarrassed, and got a smile on his face that was even bigger than the rogue-one that Slate had. "Yes, we're all *together*. Just the same. Aren't we?"

That stung, although John knew that Peter meant no harm. *Together?* They were together. John certainly wasn't. Peter was hurt and babbling. John told himself he wasn't angry, but he didn't feel "the same" as anyone right then, except maybe the losers perched at the far side of the field, the ones no school had wanted. But they'd earned their status as losers. They'd been given a chance and they didn't measure up. That was fair enough. John hadn't been given a chance. He'd worked for it, and paid for it, but it hadn't come. So what if Peter was still feeling the effects of an all-night beating? He could recuperate at any Duel School he chose. Before his conversation started to match John's bitterness, he looked over their heads, behind them, and waved at some birds circling for food. "Be right there!" he called out, as if to a friend. He stood up. "Well, I hope it works out."

"Great to meet you, Brother John," Peter said.

"Jolly times," John told him.

One of the messenger Duelists bumped into John from behind. "Pardon," she said when he turned around with a smile of acceptance on his face. She had an arm around the shoulders of Lobo Sparinada. He had his placard in his hand and tossed it to the grass, smiling. The Duelist looked up at John for a while. "So you're Brother John," she said. "Well, well. No point in talking to *you*." She and Sparinada jollied away.

"She's a Lochmann rep," Slate said. "As far as I'm concerned that takes care of Lochmann."

"Right," McMillan agreed. He looked like he would agree with anything Ben Slate thought was important. And he confirmed it. "Lochmann's out?"

"Out," Ben said.

"Out." Peter agreed. Now he looked behind him and over Ben's shoulder with an expression that was both protective and fierce. Was there anyone present who had at any time said that Lochmann Academy met any standards at all? Peter McMillan wanted to know. Their closeness made John move away, full of pain.

The food tables and the field were nearly empty three hours later. Hats were spilling out of those twelve combat circles. The visiting Duelists were in and out of the white chairs, most of them looking bored and anxious to leave, bemoaning the poor quality of this year's hopefuls in voices that carried across the space between the candidates. All along the perimeter were new

groups, hatless, segregating themselves according to
the schools they'd be attending.

The shuttles were casting longer shadows and John
was thinking longer thoughts. . . . *all but one of you.*
Clear enough, Marnie. Had everyone understood but
him? It made sense. What was added to the profession
by an oaf who was *already* unbeatable by normal standards? Duelists were people transformed. People who
looked like people anywhere. Chen Shen. A little extra
beef on the arms, but he could pass for just another useless writer. Wilkington Mosher. Could be selling anything that promised big white teeth and ladies in
swoon. Marnie durNow. Teaching your kids to say
'thank you' at the right times. No one would picture her
ripping bodies apart in a combat circle. Thus, the at-
traction. Market interest. But John looked like a fighter
and nothing else. No matter how good he might become with real training, nature would get the credit. Or
blame. No glory for any Duel School that might take
him.

I trained that fish myself. Just look at him swim!
Friend, you are a moron.

Yes, it made sense. But only from humankind's
point of view, not John's. He found himself approaching a food table, but for once he had no interest in eating. And so, with that stupid hat to cover the instrument
of his indiscretion, he pissed in the punch bowl.

The flag went down to the same blaring of horns and
freezing of bodies as before. John sat in two of the gray
chairs. Dozens of rows behind him were several hundred mostly silent ex-candidates. What's the saying?
Weeping, and gnashing of teeth. William Pfit was
there, sitting by himself. Rennie wasn't visible.

William looked up and saw John looking at him. He smiled and stood up. John shook his head and William took his seat again, looking away. John sat straight up to stay awake, knowing he'd want to sleep from the moment he got to *DOMA* until the damned thing went up in a fiery ball. That would help in a small way to express John's appreciation for life. His hands were folded neatly on his lap, knees together, hat balanced between his knees. He looked straight ahead and waited for the shuttles to start boarding.

The sun clawed at the sky until both were almost gone.

"Stand up, Brother John."

It was Marnie . . . *all but one of you* . . . durNow. Good. John hated the idea of departing Landfall with good-byes unscreamed. But the opening salvo died in his throat when he saw she wasn't alone. John popped to his feet. His hands swallowed up the hat and held it to the center of his chest. The woman standing next to Marnie was small and gray, sixtyish. She was Margaret Barrow Pritcher, as close to royalty as a human being could be.

"May I present Brother John," Marnie said. May I present what I just scraped off the bottom of my shoe. Like that. "Brother John, may I present my grandmother's cousin. Margaret durNow Barrow Pritcher." John had never heard the durNow part before.

"Very pleased, Brother John." The lady offered John her hand. Like a clod, he wiped his on his trousers before taking it.

"Duelist Barrow," he said, breathless with the words, and nodded his head.

"My name is Pritcher," she said pleasantly. "But in any case, please, call me Maggie."

"A simple courtesy would have," Marnie said, interrupting whatever John was going to mumble, "would have . . . been appreciated." She was having trouble getting the words out, as if the long streams of air coming from between her lips and I think from her ears wouldn't carry them. "When long-standing traditions are broken, one would expect—"

"Marnie," the lady said, "this needn't be unpleasant. Brother John, I'm leaving in a few minutes. I had hoped to change your mind before I go. John would be very upset if I didn't at least make the attempt."

John. She meant John Claremont Pritcher, her husband. The Colonel.

"Well?" Marnie asked stiffly.

"I . . . I . . ."

Maggie and John Pritcher, "Mom" and "Colonel" to thousands, were Lord and Lady of Mecca. Head administrators and absolute rulers of the planet called Barrow Academy.

"Well, then," Maggie said after a long silence. "I really must go now. But for the record, and for my husband. Brother John, will you come to our little school? Or won't you?"

Ordered. *Ordered* to leave me alone. 'No point in talking to *you*.' That's what she meant, the Duelist with that Lobo idiot. That's what Marnie meant by long-standing traditions being broken. That's what *everything* meant, that whole day. John couldn't stop his mind from going over and over the hours of confusion and pain when it had seemed no school would have him. He had never heard of anything like this happening before. Maybe the Pritchers were Lord and Lady of Barrow, but it was hard to imagine those other administrators taking *orders* from them? Ha! Well, they did! What could their threat have been? No more Barrow graduates for Instructors? That would do it. Whatever it was, it worked. *Hear ye, ye lesser schools,* the mighty Pritchers had proclaimed. *Hear ye, ye bottom-feeders in the lake of merit. Do not even speak to Brother John, yonder noble giant. For he is destined for Barrow Academy. Yea, so it was written before the time of his birth. He is ours.*

"Naturally, the Pritchers'll be hauled before the Duelist Union for that one. But you can bet they knew that. And they were prepared to pay the price. Any price was worth it, to get you to their little school," said Linda Doya.

"Can you imagine that?" said John, shaking his head carefully.

"Oh, yes," Linda Doya said. "I can well imagine that, Brother John. For you are indeed a noble giant, and one whose destiny must be fulfilled. The Great Domain may pass away tomorrow, but your day must come."

Maybe that isn't exactly what she said. Who knows? John was drunk as Miney's Mouse, so his memory of the conversation was never entirely clear. But she did say something.

Four of Group 33, plus one honorary member, were on the transport from Bertha Station to Barrow Academy. Four candidates getting into Barrow from one small group was thought to be a record. There was John, Ben Slate (of course), Linda Doya, Glenn

Charles, and the honorary member, Peter McMillan.
McMillan fit in so well, it wasn't long before they
thought they remembered him from the "early days" of
"Good Old 33." In fact he was the only one of them who
could get Glenn Charles to shut up, or at least to speak
like a normal human being. Part of the time, anyway.
Only Linda had anything negative to say about McMillan. Or maybe "negative" is too strong. What she said
was that Peter was hiding a "horrible, devastating secret," and that he was not what he seemed to be. Peter
was always good-natured about it, but John suspected
her teasing bothered him a little. Even so the closeness
between Linda and Peter seemed to grow every day.

The trip from Bertha to Barrow was thirty-one days.
All but a few hours of it was spent in hyperspace. It was
during the fifth day that John helped himself to Glenn
Charles's wine supply. After that he stayed steadfastly
sober and spent a lot of time looking at blank viewports.
(To say that nothing outside the ship is visible from hyperspace, is not accurate. "Nothing" is not out there, and
it wouldn't be visible if it was. The best thing to say is
that the ports are blank. And that when you're staring
out of them, people leave you alone.)

The Cunard freighter they were on carried the last
four of Barrow's eight hundred new students. The rest
had left three days before Group 33 did, on a special
charter, and would arrive three weeks ahead of them.
After paying Barrow Academy in advance for five years
of training John hadn't been able to afford the charter.
This freighter, *TRANSWAY*, was cheaper, though still
beyond his means. Fortunately the Captain was a reasonable woman. By agreeing to put on a few demon-
stration fights and handing over the remainder of his

savings, John managed to book passage. It would be nice to report that the honored of Good Old 33 traveled this way because their friend John had to. Not so. The truth is that the four of them were signed up for the charter, but Ben and Peter arrived too late to catch it. Linda wanted to travel with Ben, so she waited. Glenn Charles wanted to travel with Linda, so he did likewise. In any case, John was grateful for their company.

Except during those few hours of glorious drunkenness John was nervous. All of them were. What was about to happen to them was the real thing. Duelist training. Experts on such things have said that in the entire history of the Great Domain, and throughout human history before that, there has never been a set of secrets held for so long. Thousands of men and women had graduated from the training. Not one had ever given away the secrets to the training. Not successfully, anyway. Hundreds had died trying. That was common knowledge. There were probably hundreds of others who weren't known about. Only a few people in the enforcement arm of the Duelist Union would ever know the real numbers and stories.

All the friends knew for certain was that they had a shot at the biggest prize of all: graduation from Barrow Academy. And as Glenn Charles never tired of pointing out, the odds were against them again. Eight hundred would enter the academy. One hundred, maybe fewer, would actually graduate. Of the remaining seven hundred, his cheerful statistics promised, five hundred would die in training. Another hundred fifty would quit during the first three years, either voluntarily or because of dismissal, or because of injury. There were fifty or so from every new group of students who would just disappear. They'd be gone, and no one would ever hear from them again. According to rumor this always happened during the fourth or fifth year. The rumor said that after the third year no one was allowed to quit because by then a student knew too much. So if the Instructors decided a student wasn't likely to graduate after all, that student joined the five hundred who had an "accident." Or else became one of the fifty who just disappeared.

Training at Barrow. It was all John could think about while he was bashing the brains out, but gently, of every fool who went up against him in those exhibition fights. After ten days there were no more challenges and he spent the transit time discussing possibilities along with Ben, Peter, Linda, and Glenn Charles. They were so excited and terrified they couldn't sleep. Ben practiced round the clock, doing that "blur" trick where his arms seemed to disappear. Glenn Charles made plans to spend his fortune a hundred different ways. Linda tried to keep everyone calm. Peter fell in love with her. He seemed to be spending every moment trying to get her alone somewhere in the bowels of the ship. No matter how artsy he got about it, her answer was always the same. Just, "No!" The others were proud of her. John could barely hold down food. His weight plummeted to four hundred eighty. God, it was exciting.

When the long transit finally ended, it seemed to have gone by in half a second. Brother John's entire life felt the same way.

Down there, right outside the viewport, was a little blue and green ball called Barrow Academy.